Kit Barrie

Contents

Prelude

Once upon a time, there was an epic story of suffering and sacrifice, of magic and sorcery, and of everlasting love. It is a tale that should be shared, for any story that brings happiness is a story worth telling.

The kingdom of Thornwood was peaceful and had once been full of magic. Those born with mystical abilities were sought out and helped the country to prosper. Their skills encouraged the harvests to grow thick and bountiful. Their touch could heal those who were grievously injured. But, for reasons that no one could discern, in recent years, magic had begun to die out. Fewer and fewer babies were born with magical abilities. Those who did still possess magic found themselves in great demand as the kindly King Stephan assumed the throne. He ruled for many years, eventually taking for his wife a noblewoman named Amelia.

Queen Amelia became with child and gave birth to a boy they named Owen. He was a healthy, beautiful baby, and they were overjoyed to receive him. But Amelia had fallen ill during the pregnancy, and King Stephan was getting on in years, so they decided that Owen was to be the only child they would have. The kingdom of Thornwood was elated at the birth of Crown Prince Owen, for King Stephan was a wise and compassionate ruler, and Queen Amelia was intelligent and kind, and it was assumed that their son would inherit those same traits. But not everyone in the kingdom was delighted by the heir. Amongst the many nobles of the court was a man by the name of Raric.

Raric was a magician and a sorcerer, one of the few remaining in any of the known lands. Raric's cleverness and magical talent as a young man had not gone unnoticed by the king, and Raric was brought to the palace. He worked his way through the court, from a lowly healer to eventually becoming Stephan's closest advisor. But while his magic abilities were much lauded by the crown, unbeknownst to the king, Raric also practiced black magic. In addition to needing blood for many of its enchantments, black magic could easily corrupt the magician's soul with overuse. While healing magic restored the body and mind to its former self and encouraged what was meant to grow, black magic warped what was natural into what was not, creating transformations from that which did not exist, so it instead drew on the user's soul for power. As such, black magic had been strictly forbidden by the crown for many years and was not taught to the recent few born with magical abilities.

Raric kept his dark power and ambition hidden, feigning friendship with the king and, later, the queen, to get as close to them as possible. He had decided that when Stephan died, he would woo the fair Queen Amelia into marrying him, making him the new king of Thornwood. But he became impatient the longer Stephan was on the throne and decided to find a way to bring about the end of Stephan's reign.

The birth of Crown Prince Owen threw that plan into chaos, for Owen would inherit his father's kingdom upon the king's death, rather than Queen Amelia. In his private chambers in the palace, Raric plotted and schemed how to bring about the demise of King Stephan and Prince Owen while keeping up his pleasant façade. But Amelia suspected that Raric was not as genuine as he seemed to be, for a mother can sense when someone means to bring harm to her child. Stephan was a good king and husband, but Amelia knew that he tended to overlook signs of warning. Knowing that there would soon be visits by other royalty from around the world to celebrate the birth, Queen Amelia had the knights watch Raric more closely.

Somehow, Raric's plan was discovered and revealed to Stephan and Amelia. The guards arrested Raric for treason against the crown. He was stripped of his title as the King's Royal Advisor, and his assets were taken and destroyed. He was thrown into the dungeon to await sentencing by Stephan.

But despite the treachery committed by the dark magician, the king did not have the heart to execute someone who had once been his close friend. He instead ordered Raric banished from the kingdom. There was a small enclave of soldiers living in Ubertlund, a long trip to the north via the sea. Stephan exiled Raric to that desolate fort in the snow-filled land. Each year, the soldiers there would send a written report to Stephan to confirm the sorcerer's continued imprisonment. Many thought Stephan too kind and worried that one day Raric would return to Thornwood to seek vengeance. But years passed with no news other than his continued incarceration, and in time, Raric was all but forgotten by the people.

Across the Sapphire Sea, the kingdom of Comorra was ruled by the Monarch Elistair. While Thornwood and Comorra had been peaceful with one another for many years, there had been recent talks of uniting the kingdoms together to further the harmony and trade between them and to share knowledge more readily as magic waned in their lands. Hence, it was agreed that when children were born to the sovereigns, they would discuss a possible match. Soon after Owen's birth, Monarch Elistair visited with their two-year-old son, Ethan, and newborn daughter, Sonia.

Neither family desired to force their children into a loveless marriage, so it was decided that Owen would spend each summer in the kingdom of Comorra. Stephan and Amelia were hopeful that Owen's time with the Comorran prince and princess would cement the bonds between their kingdoms and that, in time, a loving relationship would follow. Young Ethan, for his part, took one look at the beautiful, blond baby asleep in his bassinet and promptly declared that he hated him and would prefer a puppy instead. And that was all that they saw of each other for several more years...

Chapter One

The year that Prince Owen turned six, King Stephan and his family traveled across the sea to visit Comorra. Everyone in the two kingdoms was curious to see how the meeting between the children of the mighty rulers would fare. The carriage approached the castle from the harbor, following the long path through the woods. Owen sat next to Queen Amelia on the seat, watching the trees go by in nervous anticipation.

Even at only six years old, Owen was the perfect image of his mother, with soft powder-blond hair, large blue eyes, and a slight build. He was not strong for his age, but he was quite smart and had already shown an aptitude for leadership. While still too young to understand his potential betrothal, Owen was eager to meet Princess Sonia and Prince Ethan, for there were very few children in the palace at Thornwood, and those who were there were mostly servants who either were not allowed to play with the young prince or catered to his every desire so much that he was always allowed to win. Owen was very bright and did not want to be treated in such a manner. He knew he was born to wealth and privilege, but that did not mean that he wanted everything handed to him with ease.

"Are you excited, my darling?" Amelia asked as Owen tried not to bounce on the carriage seat. The journey from the port to the castle was several hours, and Owen had grown bored of looking at trees.

Owen nodded eagerly. "But what if they don't like me?" he asked nervously, his bright blue eyes wide and worried.

"Friendship takes time," Amelia soothed. "Just be yourself."

The carriage crossed through the town surrounding the castle, over the moat's bridge, and into the large courtyard where Elistair waited with the royal court of Comorra to welcome them.

Stephan climbed out first, then helped Amelia down from the carriage, holding her hand and drawing her close once she was on the ground. Owen stepped down after them, suddenly feeling very shy. He started to hide behind Amelia's skirt, but she gave him a nudge forward toward Elistair and their children. "Go on, darling. Say hello."

Owen lifted his chin courageously, straightened up, and gave Elistair a deep bow. "Hello, Your Majesty. I am very pleased to be here."

Amelia and Stephan gave Owen a fond smile, and Elistair's eyes crinkled in delight. "A pleasure to have you in our home, Prince Owen," Elistair said, nodding their head with their elaborately decorated hair at him. "May I introduce my daughter, Princess Sonia."

Sonia stepped forward obediently, her dark pigtails bobbing. "Hello, Prince Owen. I am very pleased to meet you," she intoned formally in a way that sounded rehearsed to everyone.

"Pleased to meet you, Princess Sonia," Owen said, giving a gracious bow of his blond head. Elistair gave Sonia a pointed look, and she heaved a dramatic sigh, holding out her hand for Owen to kiss. Owen did so, giving her a beaming smile, sending titters of laughter through the assembled group at his sweetness.

"And my son, Prince Ethan," Elistair said, nudging the young man next to them.

Ethan had dark brown hair and eyes, and golden tawny skin, already significantly taller than both Owen and Sonia. Ethan bowed sulkily and held out his hand to shake as if Owen were something disgusting he had scraped off of his shoe. Owen took the hand in his and gave the back of it a kiss the way he had with Sonia. Guffaws of laughter broke out amongst the crowd. Ethan yanked his hand back, wrinkling his nose in disgust. "Blech," he said, wiping his hand on his trousers.

Elistair gave him a pointed look. "Ethan," they scolded.

Owen looked chagrined, glancing back at his mother to see if he had done something wrong, but Amelia only smiled fondly at him before turning to Elistair again. "We are so excited that the children finally have the chance to meet."

Elistair nodded and said something in return as Owen stared at Ethan, who wiped his hand on his trousers again while Sonia giggled. Neither of them looked very pleased to see him. But Owen was determined that he would make friends with the prince and princess of Comorra, as was expected of him. There had been few people he had not been able to charm with his angelic face and his sweet temperament.

"Ethan, why don't you and Sonia take Prince Owen to your playroom until dinner," Elistair suggested.

Ethan heaved a dramatic sigh like Sonia had done earlier. "Yes, Nomy." He turned and started to walk away, but Elistair made a sound through their teeth of reproachment, and Ethan turned red, facing Owen again. "Won't you please join us, Prince Owen?" he intoned flatly.

Owen glanced back at his mother and father, who both nodded encouragingly, and Owen turned back to Sonia and Ethan again. "Thank you," he said shyly. Ethan rolled his eyes and started off at a fast clip. Sonia at least waited for Owen to move to her side before following after Ethan.

The first few days, Ethan begrudgingly let Owen play with him outside in the gardens and woods, or in the parlor when he and Sonia played games in the evenings. But he soon grew very bored with him, for while Owen was smart, physical sports were not something he was skilled at. He was much more comfortable inside playing dress up or having a tea party or reading. Sonia, on the other hand, was delighted to have a playmate her own age to do those things with. They spent many hours together slaying imaginary dragons, having meetings with their royal court of plush animals, and sitting side by side to make up stories and draw them with colorful pencils.

Where Owen and Sonia's friendship blossomed, Owen's relationship with Ethan was frosty. Two years older than the blond prince, Ethan had no time for "babies." Elistair reprimanded him and told him to play with Owen, so Ethan suggested riding horses. Owen was unable to ride without the assistance of another rider, so Ethan often left him behind. More than once, Owen came back to the castle from the stable in tears.

After several days of this happening, Elistair assigned one of the palace guards, a young man named Xan, to take care of Owen when the Comorran prince went out riding. Owen was delighted, Ethan less so, as Xan followed him through the trees on his own horse, Owen securely seated on the saddle in front of him.

Owen loved animals and would bring Xan's horse, Lorenzo, sugar cubes at least once a day. Then he would sit on one of the hay bales in the stable and read. Sonia would often join him, brushing the horses and braiding their long manes and tails while Owen read aloud for the whole stable to hear. She and Owen were rarely apart that first year. Despite Elistair's admonitions that Ethan needed to be kind and spend time with Owen too, the situation did not improve, and by the end of the summer visit, Ethan was barely speaking to Owen. The tension in the air was palpable as Owen, Stephan, and Amelia returned across the sea to Thornwood.

The cold months came and went. Letters were exchanged between the noble houses, and the visit for the next year was planned. Owen was determined that this year would be better between him and the Comorran prince who was so disinterested in him. He even spent extra time at home learning how to ride a horse so he would be able to keep up with Ethan, despite not actually enjoying riding that much. He followed Sonia and Ethan around on a smaller pony, Xan following after them all on Lorenzo. But Ethan did not seem at all impressed with his riding ability, and their second summer together passed once more with awkward tension between them.

The next several years were spent with Owen and Sonia being best friends during the summer months, to the delight of their parents. Ethan tried his best to disappear around the castle when Owen was there, which led to Sonia and Owen stalking him through the corridors and grounds like spies. No matter what Owen did, it seemed that the Comorran prince was bound and determined to ignore him at every turn. Even if they tried to do something that Ethan might like, Ethan still called Owen a "baby" and would find a reason not to play with them.

Owen wasn't sure why Ethan was still so cold to him. He thought maybe it was because he was better at games of strategy, because he nearly always won. Sonia was always Owen's greatest defender, even as she grew taller and broader than the blond prince. Owen appreciated her confidence, especially around her brother. One time when he and Sonia were eleven and Ethan had said something cruel about him cheating after Ethan lost a heated game of cards, Sonia had punched her brother in the jaw. Owen had been the one to pull them apart, slightly delighted that Sonia wanted to defend his honor but also feeling incredibly bad that Sonia had laid Ethan out flat on the parlor floor. He offered his hand to Ethan to help him up from the ground, but Ethan ignored it, face burning red with anger and embarrassment. Ethan pretended Owen was invisible for the rest of the visit that year.

Chapter Two

It wasn't any better the next year, or the next. No matter what he tried, Ethan never seemed to warm up to Owen. Sonia was always there to spend time with him and call Ethan names behind his back, but Owen didn't want Ethan to be his enemy. He wanted them to be friends. Not his best friend; that was Sonia, of course, but a friend all the same.

"Why don't you like me?" Owen asked one night when Elistair finally ordered Ethan to spend time with the prince and Owen started a game of chess with him.

Ethan shrugged and shoved one of his pieces across the board. "I don't know."

"You do know," Owen said firmly. "You're always so mean to me."

"I'm not mean," Ethan defended, crossing his arms over his chest.

"I just want to be friends with you," Owen said, moving one of his pawns.

Ethan moved one of his other pieces, hardly looking at it. He then sighed and kicked his feet up onto the table, leaning back in his chair until the front legs left the floor. "All you want to do is boring stuff like read."

"Reading's not boring," Owen said.

Ethan scoffed softly. "Yeah, it is."

"Maybe you're just bad at it," Owen said.

The chair feet hit the floor again with a loud thunk. Ethan glowered at him. "I'm not bad at it. You take that back."

"No," Owen said, pushing one of his own pieces across the chess board.

Ethan let out a soft growl. "I'm just as smart as you. Smarter than you. And I can sword fight better too."

Owen let out a huff. "If you say so. It's your move."

Ethan reached across the board and snatched Owen's white king from its square, waving it triumphantly in Owen's face before shoving it into his pocket and disappearing out the parlor door. Owen sighed. He was trying so hard. It was rare that he wasn't able to charm someone with his sweet disposition and polite manners, and he didn't like it. He was determined that he and Ethan would one day be friends.

When he left that summer, Owen had the black king chess piece in his pocket, which he eventually sent back to Comorra with a letter of apology to Ethan for taking it. Ethan did not write back.

The next summer, Sonia and Owen had both turned fifteen. Sonia had developed a wide range of interests as she grew older, but one of her favorites was archery. Ethan was an accomplished archer, but Sonia outshone him in a matter of months. With her dark hair braided back, she would fire arrows on horseback at full gallop, every inch the warrior she looked. She was also skilled in swordplay and hand-to-hand combat. Owen loved to watch her practice and spar; he was not good with weapons at all. Despite Xan and some of the other guards trying their best to teach him, he was not coordinated or skilled in any sort of combat style. "I guess you'll just need a big, strong spouse to protect you," Sonia teased him one day, which made Owen blush red to the roots of his hair.

Ethan would go out to the green and shoot arrows or do sword skirmishes with the guards, throwing Owen a triumphant, slightly smug grin when he would come out the victor. Owen knew Ethan was just trying to show off, but it was still a little endearing. He made a point to applaud each of Ethan's accomplishments, and Ethan would puff out his chest and swagger away, which made Sonia roll her eyes. "You're only encouraging him," she said.

Owen giggled softly. "I know." At least he was getting Ethan's attention with the praise, which was more than he had accomplished in years. If flattery was what it took for Ethan to be friends with him, Owen was happy to encourage Ethan every chance he got.

When it came to the lavish balls Elistair would throw toward the end of their visit, Owen and Sonia often danced together. Owen might not have been skilled on the battlefield, and he was certainly overshadowed in stature by both Ethan and Sonia, but in a social situation, he was easily the center of attention. He was a talented dancer, and he loved talking with people, making everyone from servants to nobles feel like they were his equals. His laugh was often heard over the music.

"You look beautiful as ever, Princess," Owen said as he came into the ballroom that evening.

Sonia laughed and tossed her raven-dark hair. "Why, thank you, Owen," she said, smoothing the front of her fitted gown. "You look beautiful too."

Ethan made a face, then quickly dropped it as Owen turned to him. "You look very nice too, Ethan," he said, giving the prince a polite smile. "I love that jacket on you."

Ethan glanced down at the bright blue doublet, the color of the royal family of Comorra. "Thank you?" he said, then nearly jumped out of his skin as Owen reached up to brush a hair off of his shoulder.

"There, perfect," Owen said, giving Ethan a smile that was very sunny but held something behind it Ethan couldn't read. And then Owen had turned and been swallowed up by the swirling crowd again.

"He's such a flirt," Ethan grumbled to Sonia a little later that evening as he watched Owen talk with the sons and daughter of one of the visiting dukes, brushing his powder-blond hair off his forehead as he laughed at something one of them said.

"Or is he just genuinely nice, and you think that's flirting?" Sonia asked. Ethan glared at her. "Are you mad he's not flirting with you?"

"No!" Ethan said, so loudly that several people looked over at them with concern. He dropped his voice, his cheeks as red as candied apples. "I mean, he can flirt with anyone he wants to."

Sonia gave him a small, knowing smile and didn't say another word about it.

Chapter Three

Their next summer in Comorra, Sonia suddenly seemed to be quite busy. She was always flitting from practice to lessons to a dress fitting to some sort of social engagement, giving Owen a few minutes in passing before she hurried away again. Ethan wondered why Sonia's schedule had filled so quickly for the summer, especially when he had thought she was looking forward to spending time with Owen as she always did. They were rapidly approaching the age where they could be betrothed, and it was obvious that they liked each other and got along quite well. Ethan wasn't sure how to feel about that. He knew he would be happy for Sonia if she got engaged to Owen, but for some reason, the idea of that tugged at his insides with a feeling he wasn't able to identify.

Now that he wasn't attached at the hip to Sonia, Ethan started seeing Owen everywhere. They still played cards and games of strategy when the weather kept them inside, (which Owen still always won) but when it was nice, Ethan often found Owen outside by the practice green, reading a book, or playing with some of the castle hounds. Watching the floppy-eared animals jump and lick Owen's face as he laughed and taught them to sit and shake paws made Ethan's stomach tighten in an unfamiliar way.

It rained for three days in a row, so when the sun finally came out and baked the earth dry again, Ethan was more than ready for a little archery practice. He headed out to the field, only to see Owen sitting under one of the trees there, a book open on his knees as he enjoyed the sunlight. "Hi," he said.

Owen jumped and looked up at him before blushing. "Hi. I didn't hear you coming."

Ethan chuckled, holding up his bow. "Just going to try some target practice."

"May I watch?" Owen asked, tipping his head and giving Ethan a shy smile.

"If you'd like," Ethan said, feeling a slight tightness in his chest as Owen looked at him with that innocent curve of his lips. "Do you want to try it?"

Owen blinked in surprise, closing his book. "Try it?"

Ethan pointed at the target. "Have you ever tried archery before?"

Owen shook his head. "No," he said, eyes wide.

"Huh." Ethan let out what sounded like a scoff before he drew back the arrow and let it fly. It sailed across the green and struck the target, not quite dead center, but in the center circle. Owen scrambled to his feet and clapped his hands in delight.

"Wow!" he breathed. "That was amazing!"

"I know," Ethan preened, picking up another arrow and nocking it. He loosed it, and this one struck the center of the target.

Owen squealed. "Will you teach me?"

Ethan blinked in surprise. "You want to learn to shoot?"

Owen nodded, his cheeks turning pink. "I mean, if you're willing to teach me."

Ethan nodded slowly, pulling another arrow from his quiver before moving over to Owen and holding out the bow. Owen took it, finding it surprisingly light for the power behind it. Then Ethan was standing behind him, guiding his hands into position on the bow's grip. "Keep your elbow high," he said, pushing Owen's elbow up with his hand and holding it there. Owen forgot to exhale. Ethan was so close. In fact, he was pretty sure this was the closest Ethan had ever been to him. The prince was warm, smelling of fresh grass and sunshine.

Ethan wrapped his finger around Owen's on the string, helping him to draw it back. "You feel that strength?"

He certainly did. Owen's cheeks went bright pink. "Y... Yes," he breathed, wanting to suddenly let go so he could curl his fingers into Ethan's instead.

Ethan pulled his hands slowly back. "All right, release the bowstring."

Owen let it go. The arrow flopped all of four feet and hit the ground. Ethan stifled a laugh as Owen moved to retrieve it. The rest of the afternoon went similarly, with Owen nowhere even near hitting the target, even when Ethan moved it closer. He was trying as hard as he could to try to impress Ethan with even a vague mimicry of the older prince's skill, but when his arrow buried itself in the ground ten feet in front of the target for what felt like the hundredth time, Owen knew that archery was not going to be one of his talents either.

Sonia suddenly appeared on the green, carrying her own bow and quiver full of arrows. "Are you making Owen feel bad?" she asked, tossing her braided hair over her shoulder.

"Of course not," Ethan said, and Owen felt his cheeks heat at the grin Ethan gave him.

"He's a wonderful teacher. I'm a bad student," Owen said, giving Ethan a weak smile.

"You're not a bad student," Sonia said firmly. "It's just not your skillset. But that's all right. You're smart. A sharp mind is often much better than a sharp blade."

Ethan rolled his eyes at that, making both Sonia and Owen laugh. Sonia loosed an arrow, striking the center of the target down the field, and Owen clapped for her. Ethan glanced over at Owen, suddenly a little jealous that Owen was applauding for his sister now and not paying attention to him.

"Let's try something," he said suddenly to Sonia. "I bet I can catch your arrow."

Sonia and Owen both stared at him. Ethan lifted his chin, giving Owen a cocky grin. "Bet you can't," Sonia said after a moment.

"Try me!" Ethan declared.

"And get accused of murdering you when you miss it?" Sonia scoffed.

Ethan snorted. "You're the best archer in Comorra. You won't hit me on purpose."

"I don't know, I might," Sonia said, giving Owen a sly grin, and Owen laughed.

"Come on," Ethan goaded, jogging away down the green before turning to face them again.

Sonia sighed dramatically and pulled one of her arrows from its quiver. "You're my witness that it was his idea," she said to Owen.

Owen chuckled, though it was a nervous sound. Sonia was an amazing archer, as was Ethan, but that didn't mean Ethan couldn't be injured or even killed if something went wrong. He stepped aside, heart hammering, as Sonia lifted the bow with the arrow and pulled back the string. Ethan stood, tense and ready, down the green, that familiar spark of bravado in his dark brown eyes. Sonia adjusted her aim, let out an exhale, and released the arrow with a sharp twang. Owen was sure his heart stopped in his chest for a moment as the arrow sailed down the field, just past Ethan, who snatched at it and missed. The arrow struck the target a few steps behind him instead.

"Do it again," Ethan called. "I almost had it." He gave Owen a grin. "I'm going to get it this time!"

"You're not going to impress anyone if you have an arrow sticking out of your hand," Sonia said but grabbed another arrow from the quiver.

Ethan ignored her jibe as Sonia lifted the bow, aimed, and fired. The arrow skimmed past Ethan, and his fingers brushed the fletching, knocking it slightly off course, but it still struck the outer circle of the target. Sonia was already readying a third arrow, and this time, Ethan's hand closed around the very end of it, pulling it to a stop in midair.

Owen let out a whoop as Ethan held the arrow triumphantly aloft. "That was amazing!" he shouted as Ethan jogged back to them. He gave Sonia a beaming smile. "You were amazing too."

Sonia laughed and nudged him with her hip. "Thanks. That was very impressive," she said with a grin to her older brother.

"It was," Owen agreed, and Ethan's cheeks went pink. He tossed his head a bit.

"You liked that?"

"Very much," Owen said, just as the bell was rung to announce dinner.

Chapter Four

After Owen and his parents left at the end of the summer, Ethan was having trouble concentrating. He kept thinking back to Owen's bright smile when he had caught the arrow, the way his eyes lit up, the warmth between them when Ethan had been trying (and failing) to teach Owen to do archery. When the winter came and he was unable to be outside as much as he wanted, Ethan had trouble settling. He was constantly walking the hallways, into the library and picking up a book he thought Owen might like to read on his next visit and setting it aside for him. The pile in the corner grew so large that the servants brought in a brand-new shelf just for Ethan's selections.

He was on pins and needles as the colder months drew to a close and summer approached. Sonia came into Ethan's room one evening as he was getting ready for bed, flopping dramatically onto his sheets and holding out a letter in Owen's flawless penmanship. "Owen sends you his love."

Ethan jerked and turned to gape at her. Sonia laughed brightly. "Come now, brother. You don't think I saw the way you mooned over him all last summer during his visit, did you?"

Ethan swallowed hard. "I did not!"

"Oh, please. The whole court saw it," Sonia said with a roll of her dark eyes. "When are you going to propose?"

Ethan let out a strangled sound. "I've barely talked to him! He's still a kid. And besides, he's more likely to marry you."

Sonia chuckled and tossed the letter onto the bed. "Oh, Ethan, he's only two years younger than you. I don't want to marry him. He's like a brother to me. And it's clear to anyone that he only has eyes for you."

Ethan frowned. "What do you mean, it's clear to anyone?"

"The way he looks at you and talks to you," Sonia said. "The flirting, the teasing."

"What flirting?" Ethan demanded in surprise.

Sonia tossed her dark braid over her shoulder. "He spent all last summer trying to catch your attention. Did you think he was just being nice?"

He had thought exactly that. Ethan's cheeks went red, and he ducked his head so his sister would not see the embarrassment that flooded his face at the realization.

Sonia giggled. "You are so dumb," she chided. "A beautiful prince practically throws himself at your feet, and you think he's trying to make nice with you because you assume he wants to marry your sister."

"He obviously likes you," Ethan said pointedly.

"Liking someone as a friend doesn't mean you want to marry them," Sonia said. "And I have to be nice to him, as you have been nothing but a selfish jerk to him since we were kids."

"I have not!" Ethan defended, even as Sonia's words settled like lead in his stomach.

Sonia rolled her dark eyes and tossed her braid over her shoulder. "Oh, please. You have been a complete horse's ass to him from the moment you met him, and yet he still adores you. And besides, he's not my type anyway."

Ethan groaned and sank down on the bed next to Sonia. He did not want to think about Sonia having a 'type.' His sister was... well... his sister. "You think he's cute."

"Cute like a puppy," Sonia said. "He's pretty. Very pretty. And I know you like that."

Ethan wrinkled his nose. "What?"

Sonia chuckled. "You heard me. He looks like he would shatter into a million pieces if you touched him wrong, and you like being a protector."

Ethan felt a little bit of annoyance at her saying that Owen looked like he would shatter. Owen was not a piece of china or a crystal glass. He was smart, and funny, and while he was not physically very strong, he more than made up for it with his compassion and kindness. "More like you'd rip him in half," he pointed out.

Sonia laughed and tossed her braid again. "I probably would." She gave Ethan a poke in the ribs with one sharp finger. "Think about it and talk to Nomy. I think they would be supportive of that match too."

How had they gone from maybe that Ethan liked Owen to planning for them to be betrothed? Ethan flushed again. "I... I'll think about it."

Sonia nodded and gave him a quick squeeze before she bounced off the bed and left the room. The letter from Owen still lay where she had dropped it. Ethan scooped it up, opening its crinkly pages to read the letter from Owen to Sonia. It recounted his winter and the holidays at the Thornwood court and offered a few polite platitudes and inquiries. He could almost hear Owen's voice sharing the details of his time at court, the funny moments that had happened, the gossip, and how he was looking forward to his visit again in the summer. And then, at the bottom, he had written, *"Please give my warmest regards to Ethan. I look forward to seeing both of you."* Ethan felt a little flutter in his chest at that. He held the letter up to his nose, inhaling. He could almost smell Owen's skin on the pages, like honey cakes and roses. Sonia was right. He needed to talk to Elistair before the next summer visit.

The opportunity to talk to Elistair came a few days later, when Ethan met with them in their chambers as Elistair prepared for the day, holding still for one of the servants to do up their long, raven-dark hair in an elaborate twist.

"Nomy," he asked, addressing Elistair in the way he and Sonia had always referred to their parent as children. "How terrible would it be if Prince Owen didn't marry Sonia?" He scuffed the toe of his boot into the carpet to avoid having to look into Elistair's eyes.

Elistair glanced over at him. "Do you have reason to think that he will not?"

Ethan sighed, his cheeks going red. "Well, uh…"

Elistair smiled gently. "Tell me your thoughts."

Ethan bit his lower lip thoughtfully. "I... I just feel that, this last summer, Owen and I... got closer, and..."

Elistair waited patiently, but when Ethan went silent, they added, "Do you like him, my dear?"

Ethan's cheeks went red, and he ducked his head. "I don't know."

"I think you do," Elistair said, not unkindly, catching Ethan's eyes in the mirror again. "Do you want him to marry Sonia?"

Ethan cleared his throat. "I wouldn't want him to be unhappy, or for our country's treaty with Thornwood to fall through."

"Do not worry about the treaty," Elistair soothed. "This is about you, and Owen, and Sonia."

Ethan flushed, staring at the ground as he dug his toe into the carpet again. "I would be happy if Owen married Sonia because... because I want him around."

"But you would like it more if he married you?" Elistair prompted.

Ethan's shoulders slumped. "I don't know. Marriage is a big step."

"It is," Elistair said. "One that should not be taken lightly, for any decision we make will impact our people and our country."

"How did you know you didn't want to get married, Nomy?"

Elistair was thoughtful for a moment before replying, "I never found someone I loved enough that I wanted to spend the rest of my life with them. Marriage is not for everyone." They gave Ethan a smile. "Have you spoken to Owen about any of this?"

"No," Ethan said, voice too loud and quick to sound casual about it.

"Perhaps you should," Elistair said. "When he visits this summer, spend some time with him. See how you feel, and how he feels as well. No formal proposals have been made."

Ethan brightened a little at that. He hopped down from his seat on the bed, moving over to kiss Elistair on the cheek. "Thank you, Nomy," he said. "I will! I'll tell Owen how I feel!"

Elistair beamed at him in the mirror. "Of course, my dear."

Ethan frowned thoughtfully. "What if he doesn't like me?"

"Then it is his loss," Elistair replied, placing a hand on Ethan's and squeezing gently.

Chapter Five

Summer couldn't come quickly enough, and yet it came too fast for Ethan. He wasn't sure if it would be better if Owen liked him or if he rejected him outright. Sonia was completely uninterested in marrying Owen, and, from what he could tell, Owen's feelings for Sonia were entirely platonic as well. If their marriage did not happen, and Ethan didn't speak up, Owen might never come to visit again, and that thought made his heart ache. He tried not to bounce as he waited in the courtyard for the approaching royal carriage. He had no idea how to declare his love to Owen; hopefully a moment would naturally occur that would allow him to say something.

The carriage pulled to a stop inside the castle courtyard. When the doors opened, Owen stepped out first, and Ethan caught his breath. Despite having traveled for days, Owen was beautiful, his blond hair perfectly in place, his pale skin glowing. He gave Ethan and Sonia a bright smile before he turned and offered his hand to his mother, and Amelia stepped down carefully from the carriage. Stephan followed after her, and Amelia took his arm. Even after all of these years, the love between them was obvious, and Ethan felt a stab of envy. He wondered if one day Owen would look at him like that.

"Welcome," Elistair said with a gracious smile to all of them.

Owen stepped forward, giving a bow to Elistair, then taking Sonia's hand, giving it the required kiss. "Hello, Princess," he said politely.

"Hello, Prince Owen," Sonia said back, her voice its usual formal greeting.

Owen turned to Ethan, and they stared at each other for a long moment. Both of them had filled out a bit more in the past year. Owen was still the slender, graceful youth, but the gawkiness of his limbs seemed to have gone away, and his eyes, though still large, no longer looked too wide for his delicate face. Ethan had packed on more muscle this year, his shoulders wider, his jaw a little firmer, still almost a foot taller than the petite blond.

Owen gave Ethan a smile that looked polite, but Ethan could see something in Owen's gaze as he stared at him. A sort of shyness, tinged with hope. "Hello, Prince Ethan."

"H... Hello." Ethan's voice came out much too high as he greeted him, not moving. Owen held out his hand to Ethan, and Ethan stared at it for several very long seconds of silence that stretched on through the courtyard.

Owen's face fell just a bit, and he started to pull his hand back before Ethan realized that he had not returned the gesture. He quickly thrust out his hand, snatching Owen's, and, before he could think about it, bowed and brought his lips to the back of Owen's hand, brushing them over it the way Owen had with his sister.

Owen let out a soft squeak, his cheeks going bright pink as he stared at Ethan in surprise, his pale fingers curling into Ethan's golden ones. Ethan lifted his head again, his own face red as he realized what he had done. Someone tittered, and the awkward silence was broken by laughter from the observers as the two princes held each other's gazes.

Elistair raised their hands with a smile. "I trust your journey was not unpleasant."

"It was very nice," Stephan said, and the three leaders began to talk as Ethan realized he was still holding Owen's hand. He jerked his hand back and cleared his throat, giving Owen a lopsided grin. Owen stared at him for another long moment, the pink still tinging his cheeks as his blue eyes held Ethan's dark brown ones.

"I'm sure you would like to freshen up before dinner," Elistair was saying, and servants began unpacking the carriage.

Owen gave Ethan and Sonia a small smile before letting himself be led to his guest chamber, still feeling the petal-soft brush of Ethan's lips on the back of his hand.

Dinner was a lavish affair to welcome the Thornwood royal family, and then they all retired early, for travel was long and arduous. Ethan kicked himself for not finding time to speak to Owen when all he wanted to do was blurt out his feelings. But he tried to reassure himself that Owen would be more receptive to him after a good night of sleep and was determined to find time to speak with him the next day.

His first chance came in the early afternoon, after luncheon had been served, and Owen sat in the castle library, reading something as he sat curled on one of the large, comfortable chairs. He looked so peaceful that Ethan almost didn't want to disturb him. But he thought if he did not speak up soon, his heart would fly into his throat and choke him to death. So, he pasted on a confident smile and strode over to the blond prince. "Hello, Owen."

Owen glanced up and smiled at him, a slightly nervous but genuinely sweet look that made Ethan's stomach tighten. "Hello, Ethan."

"Can I talk to you?" Ethan asked, trying very hard not to fidget with his clothes.

"Of course." Owen set his book aside and sat up, looking expectant.

"Alone?" Ethan asked, glancing around the room at the guards, servants, and nobles.

Owen blinked, then gave him a small grin. "Am I in trouble?"

"No!" Ethan said, a little too loudly, and everyone in the room turned to look at him. He blushed bright red, ducking his head.

"I'm just teasing," Owen soothed, rising to his feet. "Shall we walk in the gardens?"

At least if Owen turned him down in the gardens, there would be plenty of bushes for him to run and hide in. Ethan nodded, turning on his heel to lead the way, aware of all eyes following both him and Owen out of the room. The guards trailed them until they reached the beautifully laid out garden pathways, then hung back a little to give the princes an illusion of privacy.

"Shall we sit?" Owen asked, gesturing to one of the stone benches. But Ethan was too anxious to sit, shifting from foot to foot. Owen frowned slightly. "What's wrong?"

"Nothing's wrong," Ethan said, trying to smile, but his whole face felt paralyzed.

"What did you want to talk about then?" Owen asked, sitting down cautiously on the edge of the bench. Ethan was making him nervous, staring at him so intensely with that dark gaze.

"I... I was talking to Nomy," Ethan started. That seemed like a safe way to approach this conversation. "About you and Sonia."

"What about us?" Owen said, his voice going suddenly softer.

"Are you going to marry her?" Ethan asked.

Owen blinked in surprise at the blunt question. "I don't know," he said thoughtfully. Ethan could hear the uncertainty in his voice, as if he were trying to not say anything that might offend Ethan or give him cause to defend Sonia's honor. "She is my best friend. Did you want me to ask your permission first?"

"No," Ethan said quickly. "You don't need my permission to marry my sister." He could almost hear Sonia's laughter in his head at the thought that she needed her brother's permission to do anything at all.

"Then what is it?" Owen asked.

Ethan cleared his throat. This suddenly felt like a terrible idea, and he had never been so afraid in his life. He wanted to turn and run, which he knew was foolish. This was Owen, who was the most gentle, compassionate person he had ever known. His fingers twisted nervously in his tunic, and he felt a few embroidered threads snap. "Sonia told me that... that last year you were flirting with me all summer, and I didn't notice."

"Oh." Owen's cheeks went bright pink, and he ducked his head. "I... I'm sorry. It wasn't meant to be a slight against your sister or anything."

"So, you were? Flirting with me?" Ethan asked, his mouth suddenly very dry.

Owen curled up on himself a little more. "Yes."

"Why?"

"Why what?"

"Why were you flirting with me?"

Owen felt his heart twinge inside of him. "Because it's you," he blurted out, feeling his face go red and clapping his hands to his cheeks as if to hold back the embarrassment.

Ethan gaped at him. "It's me, what?"

"I like you," Owen said, forcing the words out before he choked on them. He stared at Ethan, waiting for the young man to slap him, or tell him he was not interested in men, or tell him to leave his kingdom and never return. But Ethan did none of that. In fact, he didn't even really do anything, just gazed back at Owen in silence, his mouth slightly agape.

The silence stretched between them, tense as a bowstring. Owen's cheeks grew hotter each moment until he was afraid he would start bleeding out of his nose for all the blood rushing to his face. "I... I'm sorry," he said, feeling like his heart was about to crack from the pressure. Whatever Ethan had to say to him, he could be a man and take it. Ethan at least deserved that much after that unexpected announcement.

Ethan was looking so hard at him, as if searching for something. "You... like me?" His voice was so breathy and uncertain, as Owen had never heard it before.

"Yes," Owen said, unsure what else he could say, since he was not about to lie to Ethan about what he had just said.

"And you don't want to marry Sonia because... you want to marry me?" Ethan asked.

Owen frowned, realizing he had not really thought that far into the future. He hadn't dared to hope that Ethan might return his feelings, so marriage had rarely crossed his mind. "I... I don't know," he said.

There was another long, tense silence, before Ethan suddenly dropped to one knee in front of the bench so he could look up into Owen's face. "I like you too," he said softly. It felt much easier to say now that Owen had admitted it first.

"You do?" Owen couldn't hide his surprise. "You didn't seem like you did last year."

Ethan flushed a little. "I didn't realize you were flirting. And it seemed like you loved Sonia, so I wasn't going to get in the way of that."

Owen let out a breathy laugh. "So, we've been dancing around each other for years?"

"No. I really didn't like you when we were kids," Ethan admitted. Owen stared at him for a long moment before he began to laugh, doubling over as he held his sides. And then both of them were laughing until tears rolled down their faces.

"We are quite the pair," Owen said when the laughter had finally abated.

Ethan swiped at his own face to clear the tears off of them. "We really are," he agreed.

Chapter Six

After that, Ethan and Owen were almost always together. Owen would take a book outside to the practice fields while Ethan would spar or shoot archery. Once in a while, Owen would try some sword play or attempt to shoot a bow and arrow, but he was still not good at it, nor did he really enjoy it. "It's okay," Ethan had told him once after Owen became frustrated that he had not made any progress in sword fighting after several hours of practicing the same motions over and over. "You can think circles around me."

That did seem to be true. Owen was clever; he and Sonia often played games of strategy. Sonia only rarely was able to best him, and none of them could remember a time when Ethan had ever won any sort of strategic game against either of them. Sonia had also made it a habit, when she did spend time with the princes this summer, to disappear after an hour or so, leaving them alone once more. Owen found it hilarious. Ethan didn't understand how Sonia was always so busy now, and Owen decided to just let him figure it out on his own.

"Meet me in the library tonight at midnight," Ethan told Owen one evening after dinner as the nobles gathered in the parlor, giving him a smile that he meant to be cocky, but he could hear the uncertainty in his own voice. "We can have some fun."

Owen's cheeks went red. "What kind of fun?" he asked.

Ethan grinned. "It's a secret," he said conspiratorially. "Just don't wear really nice clothes."

Owen almost choked on nothing, staring at Ethan as his mind went to all of the places it shouldn't have. What could they possibly be doing, that he shouldn't wear nice clothes? He quickly turned away with a nod. "Midnight," he agreed and hurried away before Ethan could see the redness coloring his cheeks.

Once the servants had departed from his room for the night, Owen slipped from under his covers, pulling on a plain white blouse and black trousers and boots. But he felt underdressed for anything, even if it might only be him and Ethan, so he added a simple brown damask waistcoat on top of it. He grabbed his dressing robe to throw over it before opening the door to his room. Two guards stood watch on either side of the door.

"Your Highness?" one of the guards asked in concern, studying him intently.

Owen gave her a charming smile, the kind he always had for everyone. "I'm afraid I'm having trouble sleeping," he said. "I was going to go to find a book to read."

"Of course," the guard said, nodding to her companion to stay at the chamber door before gesturing politely. "I will escort you there."

"Thank you." Owen headed for the library, the guard trailing after him. The library doors were closed, and he opened one with a creak that sounded very loud in the stillness of the castle. "I will be all right from here," he said, and the guard nodded, taking up sentry next to the doorframe.

Owen slipped inside. The library was dark, but after he had closed the door and lit one of the candles from the table nearby, he could see a similar glow toward the back of the room. He followed it, carefully skirting the furniture and shelves. "Ethan?" he whispered loudly into the darkness.

He turned a corner, and Ethan was standing in front of a large, open wall panel, holding a lantern that cast a warm, yellow glow over him and made his shadow dance. "You came!" he said eagerly.

Owen nodded, glancing at the open panel that looked to be a hidden passage. "What is this?"

"We're going into town," Ethan said with a beaming smile, and Owen froze in surprise.

"We're what?"

"We're going into town," Ethan repeated, holding out his hand. "Come on!"

"Don't we need guards to go with us?" Owen asked, biting his lower lip in concern.

"I can handle myself," Ethan said, lifting up the edge of the cloak he wore to reveal a sword strapped to his hip. "Come on!" He held up a second cloak to Owen.

Owen hesitated for just a moment before he blew out his own single candle and shed his dressing gown. He took the cloak Ethan offered him, obviously one of his own that nearly touched the ground on his shorter frame. He set his robe and candle on a nearby chair, then moved over to Ethan's side. His heart fluttered in his chest, realizing that this was the first time he had ever been completely alone with Ethan in the entire time they had known one another. No guards watching them, no courtiers or servants around; just them, and the yawning, dark hole of the open wall.

Ethan grabbed Owen's hand and gave him a tug as he ducked into the open panel. Owen followed carefully after him, Ethan's lantern illuminating a stone passageway. Ethan pulled the library panel shut, then took Owen's hand to guide him, holding the lantern aloft to throw its feeble light into the extended darkness.

"We'll be in so much trouble if our parents find out," Owen whispered, pulling his cloak tighter around him.

Ethan laughed. "Trust me, no one will find out. I do this all the time."

"All the time?" Owen asked in surprise.

"Yeah," Ethan said, giving his hand a squeeze. "Don't worry. I'll protect you."

That phrase sent warmth through Owen's body, his step faltering just enough that Ethan looked back to catch his eye. Owen beamed at him before hurrying to keep up with Ethan's longer strides. The pathway was so dark, the only other illumination being from a few cracks under the false walls they passed. Their hands mingled warmth as they hurried along.

Owen was just beginning to wonder if Ethan actually knew where he was going when Ethan came to a stop, turning and holding the lantern out to Owen. "Here."

Owen took it, then watched as Ethan found a few hidden handholds built into the rocky walls. He braced his shoulder against the ceiling of the passage and pushed upward with a grunt. A square of light appeared above him. He pushed it harder, and a trap door appeared, tipping back on its hinges. Ethan jumped up to grab the edge of the hole and pull himself out, scrambling on the ground as he did, which got dirt all over his clothes. Owen wrinkled his nose in distaste but also realized that he was not going to be able to jump and grab the edge the way Ethan had, as Ethan was much taller and stronger than he was.

Ethan suddenly laid flat on the ground, offering his hand down to Owen. "Come on."

Owen gazed at the hand in confusion. "What?"

Ethan curled his fingers. "Grab my hand, I'll pull you up."

Owen frowned. "I know you're strong, but I don't think you can pull me all the way up."

"Try me," Ethan said with a grin.

Owen glanced at the lantern uncertainly. "Just leave that here, we can see fine with the moon," Ethan offered.

Owen set the lantern aside, then turned his gaze above him again. "This seems like a bad idea."

Ethan chuckled. "You can blame it all on me." Owen frowned, but he stretched up and took Ethan's hand. "Jump on three," Ethan said. Owen barely had time to process that when Ethan counted, and Owen gave an awkward little hop. His feet left the ground, his arm and shoulder aching as Ethan pulled, then wrapped a second hand around his wrist and hauled him up onto the grass. Owen was glad he was not wearing his nice clothing as he bumped against the edge of the trap door, staining his shirt as he grabbed at the earth with his free hand. Ethan was on his knees now and suddenly gave a sharp tug; Owen found himself flying up and forward, crashing into Ethan, and both of them went tumbling backward onto the grass of the palace gardens. Ethan landed on his back, holding Owen to his chest. He grunted as he hit the ground, the air leaving his lungs in a whoosh.

Owen landed on top of him, barely avoiding kneeing Ethan in the groin, their faces inches apart.

"Sorry," Owen gasped.

"It's all right." Ethan grinned, then reached up to brush a lock of Owen's blond hair behind his ear. "You look so pretty with the stars behind you," he commented.

Owen blinked at that. "Um… thank you."

"Uh huh."

"You're really strong," Owen ventured shyly.

"Thank you." Ethan puffed out his chest a bit before shifting to help Owen sit up and disentangle himself from his cloak. He got to his feet, brushing off his own clothes, then held out a hand to help Owen up from the ground.

Owen glanced around as he rose to his own feet on legs that were not entirely steady after his launch through the trap door. The hidden opening was in the palace gardens, and he could see now that there was a large pedestal vase full of flowers on top of it. Ethan reached down to pull the vase upright and close the trap door again under it. It disappeared into the green grass, and Owen took a moment to admire Ethan's muscles flexing as he settled the pedestal in place. "I can barely see that," he said, motioning to the hidden passage entrance.

Ethan grinned and shoved his hair out of his face, leaving a streak of dirt across his forehead. "Most people don't know about it. It's meant as an escape for the royal family in case of an emergency." He pointed to a nearby stone lantern. "Two down from that," he said, indicating the second planter in the row that hid the trap door. "In case you ever need to use it." He reached up to brush his thumb over Owen's lower lip, which might have been romantic if his hands weren't covered in dirt, and Owen made a face at the streak left on his face.

"But you use it to go into town?"

"Of course," Ethan said with a shrug, as if it were an everyday occurrence for a prince to leave the palace unescorted. "Don't you have something like that at your home?"

"Yes, but I don't sneak out," Owen said with a slight harumph.

Ethan laughed brightly. "I might just corrupt you, then, Your Highness."

Ethan's words sent a shiver through him, and Owen pulled his cloak tighter as a strange heat crept down his back. "I'll allow it," he said, giving the words an extra bit of royal haughtiness.

Ethan grabbed his hand. "Come on! Let's go before someone sees us!" He pulled Owen along through the garden, keeping low and away from the lit lanterns until they reached the stone wall that encompassed the palace grounds. There was a small wrought-iron gate, and Ethan slipped a key from his pocket to unlock the gate and motion Owen through before he locked it again behind them. They crossed over one of the small bridges that spanned the moat, and then they were outside the confines of the castle, the kingdom of Comorra stretched out before them. Ethan took Owen's hand and gave him a pull down one of the cobbled streets. Owen trotted after him, blue eyes wide as he looked around.

The streets were narrower than he had realized from driving through them in a carriage, the houses and shops packed closely together, and Owen learned very quickly to watch his step to avoid horse droppings and piles of trash that had not been fully swept from the path. Windows gleamed like diamonds, raucous shouts of laughter emanating from one of the buildings they passed as people spilled from its inviting warmth into the night. "You do this all the time?"

"Yeah," Ethan gloated. He had not originally planned to let Owen in on his secret, but there was something that made him want to be alone with the other prince, to spend time with him without someone watching their every move. "Do you want a drink?" he asked as they came to a stop in front of a brightly-lit tavern window.

Owen blinked. "Um, sure?"

Ethan beamed. "I'll get you something you'll like. Come on." He pushed open the door. Music was being played by a three-person band in the corner, and people were sitting or standing around, talking and laughing. The air was warm and heavy with the smell of ale and bread and sweat. Owen found himself clinging a bit tighter to Ethan's hand as they walked. He had met peasants before but always in his official capacity as a prince. Tonight, they were not princes. No one recognized them or bowed to them; they were just anonymous faces in the drunken crowd.

"Wait right here." Before Owen had a chance to even process what Ethan had said, Ethan had let go of his arm and disappeared into the crowd around the bar. Owen stood awkwardly in the middle of the tavern floor, suddenly feeling very small and alone. People moved around him with barely a glance; he was used to having the eyes of servants and soldiers on him constantly. No one apologized if they bumped him or stepped on his toes. The press of bodies so close to him made his skin prickle with heat under Ethan's warm cloak. He played nervously with the edge of it as he watched the people converge and recede. It was like a dance at a ball, though one much louder and without the same grace. He was not as familiar with the people of Comorra as he was those in Thornwood. He would go out with his mother when the queen did charity work. Perhaps he could do more of it, learn more about the common people beyond only the exceptionally downtrodden. One day he would be king, after all, and he wanted to be a good king. And perhaps, one day, he might also rule Comorra by Ethan's side. That thought made his cheeks warm just a little.

A few people jostled him as they passed, and Owen did his best to stay out of the way until a hand landed on his shoulder, squeezing uncomfortably tight. Owen turned to see a large, bearded man, eyes red, breath stinking of booze as he looked blearily at Owen.

"How much?" the man asked, reaching down to pinch Owen's cheek roughly.

"How much what?" Owen asked, his own hand sliding up to push the man's touch away from his face.

"How much for me to take you upstairs?" the man asked.

Owen's eyes narrowed into a glower. "I'm not for sale."

"You mean I can have it for free?" the man said with a leer, sliding his arm around Owen's waist to pull him close against his thick chest.

"Unhand me," Owen said, glancing around for Ethan, but the other prince had vanished in the sea of people.

"Come on, beautiful, everyone's got a price," the man said.

"You can't afford him," came a voice nearby, and Owen nearly melted in relief as he turned his head to see Xan standing right behind him, dressed in his captain's armor he had earned two years ago.

The drunk man's face paled as he saw the royal insignia on the man's chest. Captain Xan raised a brow. "Walk away, before I make you."

The man turned and hastily disappeared into the crowd, shoving people out of his way as he staggered.

Owen turned to Xan, biting his lower lip nervously. "Thank you, Captain. What are you doing here?"

"Prince Ethan has been sneaking out a lot at night to go into town, so I've been keeping an eye on him," Xan replied, nodding toward a corner, and Owen obediently trailed him. "This is his favorite tavern to visit, so I figured it was where he would be when the guards realized you were both gone."

Owen frowned. "I'm sorry. Are we in trouble?"

Xan opened his mouth to answer before Ethan suddenly appeared at Owen's side with two cups of cider, looking a little pale as he saw Xan. "Captain, what are you doing here?"

"I might ask you the same question, Your Highness," Xan said, keeping his voice low.

Ethan frowned. "I wanted to spend some time with Owen."

"You still need to be escorted," Xan replied.

"I can take care of myself," Ethan huffed.

"Yes, Your Highness, but it's still required," Xan said. "And, while I know you can defend yourself, leaving Prince Owen to fend for himself in a place like this is not the wisest decision. He could have been hurt."

Ethan frowned. "I wouldn't let that happen."

"He was just accosted," Xan replied with a slightly exasperated look. "What if that had been an assassin?"

"I'm standing right here," Owen pointed out as the two men bickered over his inability to defend himself. He did not want to be the reason Ethan was in trouble, nor did he want to cause issues for the guards who were supposed to be watching them.

Captain Xan sighed. "You may stay out, Your Highnesses, but I am staying with you, for your own protection."

Ethan looked like he wanted to protest, but Owen quickly held up his hand and gave Xan a gracious smile. "Thank you, Captain, we accept," he said.

Ethan groaned in frustration as they sat down at a table, Xan standing a bit away. "I wanted a night without having people watching us."

"It's all right," Owen said, taking the mug handed to him and clinking it to Ethan's. "We can still have fun."

Ethan looked sulky, but he drank the cider, and then he and Owen got into a spirited game of cards with some people at another table that ended with Owen winning nearly every hand but then giving all of his coins back to the individuals at the end of the night. "It's not right to take their money from them when I have no need for it," he explained to Ethan as they walked back toward the palace, Xan following behind them. The sun was barely peeking up over the horizon, painting the sky in bright pinks and oranges.

Ethan caught Owen's hand and gave it a squeeze. "You're just too nice."

Owen giggled. "I try to be. I want to be a good king to my people when the time comes."

Ethan nodded thoughtfully. "Do you think... we might join our kingdoms together?"

Owen was silent for a moment before turning his sapphire eyes to Ethan's mahogany ones. "You mean, will we get married one day?"

Ethan flushed and gave an attempt at a nonchalant shrug, but Owen could see the nervousness behind it. "Maybe."

"I don't know. I mean, we've only really just started spending time together," Owen offered, giving his hand another gentle squeeze. "But I do like you."

"I like you too," Ethan said, pausing mid-stride as Owen suddenly pulled him to a stop.

"May I kiss you?" Owen asked quietly, and Ethan blinked in surprise.

"Um... sure," he said, his heart picking up in his chest.

Owen slowly leaned in, his hands moving to Ethan's shoulders, and their mouths met in a shy kiss. Ethan's own hands slid up to hold Owen's waist. It was just as he had imagined it, sweet and innocent and perfect. Just like Owen. And, like children getting their first taste of summer strawberries, they wanted more, hands clutching one another greedily as lips met again, hungry and lost to the world. Breath ghosted over skin as they kissed, drawing closer each moment until they were nearly entwined in one another's arms. Owen finally pulled away with an embarrassed groan, glancing back at Xan, who was politely watching them without watching them. "We should stop."

Ethan tried not to pout, his lips swollen from the ferocity of Owen's mouth on his. "We should," he agreed.

Owen stepped back, straightening his clothes, his cheeks stained as red as roses. "Does your Nomy and Sonia know that you... like me?"

Ethan chuckled. "I think everyone knew except me."

Owen flushed and ducked his head. "Oh."

"I don't think it's an issue with the uniting of our kingdoms," Ethan ventured. "So, if it's all right with you... I'd like to court you."

Owen giggled. "You would?" he asked hopefully.

Ethan nodded. "Is that all right?" Owen hummed and pretended to think. Ethan gave him a poke in the ribs. "Very funny."

Owen snickered and leaned in to give Ethan one more kiss. "How could I say no to such a polite request?"

The rest of the summer held stolen romantic moments, pushing each other into dark corners or hedgerows to kiss. Xan made Ethan promise not to sneak out again without guards to accompany them, and Owen made him stick to that promise, no matter how much Ethan groused about the lack of privacy or wanting time alone with Owen.

Of course, not all of the time spent in Comorra was fun and games. Owen and Ethan and Sonia traveled the area, doing charity work, visiting the farmsteads and the ports, and attending various functions and celebrations for some of the aristocratic families. There were also meetings with various royal advisors, town leaders, and noble dignitaries.

One of the topics that often came up was the lack of people being born with magical abilities. Thornwood had seen none in the most recent years, and Comorra's numbers had sharply declined to almost zero as well. There did not seem to be a reason for the loss of magic, nor did anyone know how to stop it. Some knowledge of healing and the cultivation of crops had already been lost in the time before anyone realized how dire the situation had become. Stephan, Amelia, and Elistair, along with their children and various government officials, discussed how to ensure that farmers and physicians were supported and trade maximized. The kingdoms would have to work closely together to be certain the health of the lands and their people continued to prosper without magic.

Funding had been allocated to several universities for more physicians to study, but there was still the concern of knowledge that was being lost as magic users died. It was Owen who suggested to the assembly that magicians who were still alive be compensated for recording their knowledge in written form so it could be compiled and organized. The pride shining in Ethan's eyes as the officials approved moving forward with the plan made Owen's heart flutter.

The time came too quickly for Owen and his parents to return to Thornwood. Owen and Ethan parted with kisses and promises to write letters until they were able to see each other again next year. Owen wrote at least once a week to Ethan, though he received far fewer letters in return.

Chapter Seven

Owen was eager to arrive at the castle in Comorra the following summer. He wondered if Ethan might propose to him. Not that they would get married right away, of course; as princes with their own kingdoms, there would be many details to work out. And while they had spent the previous summer so close to one another, the words "I love you" had not yet been exchanged between them, either in word or in writing. Owen thought he loved Ethan, and he was pretty sure Ethan felt the same in return, but there was still the bashfulness of a new relationship, despite them having known one another for many years now.

"There's no need to rush anything, my darling," Amelia had said as the carriage approached the castle and Owen toyed nervously with the hem of his waistcoat. "If it was meant to be, it will happen." She gave Stephan a loving look across the small space.

Stephan smiled back at her, giving her knee a squeeze. "Your mother is right, my boy. Just enjoy your time together."

"How did you know when you loved each other?" Owen asked curiously.

"I knew I loved your mother the moment I first saw her," Stephan said. "It was at a dinner party, and even with a thousand people in the room, I only saw her."

Amelia giggled. "He was such a charmer," she said, giving Stephan a loving wink. "He sent me flowers every day for a month, and a poem to go with each one."

"They were terrible," Stephan admitted with a chuckle.

"They were, so terrible," Amelia agreed, and both of them burst into fits of laughter at the memory. Owen beamed. He wondered if he and Ethan would find love together the way his parents had. Just thinking of seeing Ethan made his heart swell and butterflies flutter in his stomach. He thought that could be love. Did Ethan feel the same when he thought of him?

The carriage pulled to a stop inside the palace gates, and Owen forced himself to wait patiently until he could alight with grace and poise, as was expected of him. He looked over and found Ethan immediately, standing next to Elistair, looking even broader and stronger than he had last year, his dark eyes bright, his golden skin accenting his jawline from the sun. He was stunning, and Owen had to keep back an audible inhale, instead putting on a warm smile. He greeted Sonia first, who looked as elegant as any lady he had ever seen, her hair piled into a beautiful design on top of her head, woven with gold silk ribbons. She greeted him with her usual formality, but he could see the mischievous glint in her eyes that she had just for him. He turned to Ethan, his heart giving an extra beat in his chest. "Hello, Ethan."

Ethan grinned at him. Owen still looked radiant, his shoulder-length white-gold hair falling in light curls, his milky skin glowing in the sunlight. "Hi," he said, wanting to fold Owen into his arms and kiss him senseless, but they were in the middle of the courtyard, and it was not appropriate. So, he just gave Owen a bow. "I've missed you."

"I've missed you," Owen said wistfully in return.

He had hoped that things would go back to the way they had been when he had left at the end of last summer. The stolen kisses around every corner, the gentle touches, sweet side-glances, and flirtatious smiles. Instead, the very first night after dinner, Ethan asked Owen if he wanted to go hunting with him the next morning. That was not Owen's idea of fun, but he reluctantly agreed. "I don't know that I could shoot anything," he ventured.

"That's okay," Ethan assured him with a bright grin and a kiss to his cheek. "I'll get it if you don't." Owen bit his tongue to keep from responding that that was not what he had meant; the thought of shooting an arrow into anything other than a straw target made his stomach clench. But Ethan looked so hopeful that he didn't want to deny him. And it would give them some time to be together. But, after they made camp in the forest the next day and went out on their horses looking for game, the first arrow of Ethan's that found its mark in a fox made Owen burst into tears.

"I know it's what happens," he sobbed as Ethan held him close, at a loss for what else to do.

"You have a good heart, Your Highness," said Xan, who had accompanied Ethan on their hunting trip. "You don't like seeing things suffer."

"But it didn't," Ethan protested, for he had shot the creature quite skillfully. Xan gave him a pointed look, and for once, Ethan shut his mouth and let the captain soothe over the situation. Owen hung back with a few of the other servants, much happier to help prepare the evening meal. The servants were more than understanding and distracted him with stories and songs and court gossip. Despite being a prince, everyone in the Comorran court loved Owen, for he was friendly and charming and wanted to be helpful, even if it was not his duty to do so.

Xan made sure he and Ethan had all of the carcasses dressed and broken down away from camp, returning with the meat ready for cooking. Owen happily nestled against Ethan's side as they ate a delicious meal of stewed deer, the fox meat being salted and dried. They were going to go out again in the morning, and Ethan and Owen curled up together in a nest of furs and pillows in a tent.

"Are you doing okay now?" Ethan asked as he folded Owen awkwardly into his arms in what Owen assumed was meant to be a comforting embrace.

"Yes," Owen said. "Thank you. I'm sorry if I spoiled your trip."

"It's fine," Ethan said, holding him close under the warm blanket. Owen curled up against his side. "Ethan?" he asked.

"Hmm?" the dark-haired prince said against his skin.

"I missed you."

"I missed you," Ethan replied, leaning up to kiss him softly, stroking his fingers into Owen's blond hair. He pressed another kiss to his lips before his eyes closed, and he nestled into the bed of pillows, cuddling Owen against him in the darkness.

The next morning, Ethan was up before dawn and carefully extricated himself from a sleeping Owen to go wash up and dress before he and Xan and a few others went out hunting again. Owen woke up alone in the bed, Ethan's spot having gone cold by the time his eyes opened. That was disappointing; he wished Ethan had woken him to let him know he was heading out. But he knew Ethan loved hunting, so he was not about to protest. He got ready for the day, helped the servants prepare lunch for when the hunters came back, then packed up the camp.

Ethan returned with another deer, several foxes, and a rabbit, all of which he at least had the decency to keep out of Owen's line of sight until the meat and hide were separated and no longer looked like freshly-killed animals. After a quick lunch, the group returned to the palace, and Ethan left Owen on his own so they could both go bathe after being out in the woods for two days. Xan did come by later that day to ask Owen if he was doing all right. Owen was slightly embarrassed that he had been so tender-hearted in front of the captain who had watched him grow up all of these years, but Xan only smiled in reassurance and promised there would be no more hunting trips that involved Owen.

Chapter Eight

Their routine of Ethan going outside to practice and Owen sitting nearby with a book continued, as it had the previous years, but Owen found himself captivated as he watched Ethan shoot arrows or spar with Sonia or the guards. Ethan moved with a sort of precision and grace that Owen admired, though he found himself watching Sonia just as often as he watched Ethan. Sonia was an extremely accomplished fighter herself, and more than once Owen cheered for her as she knocked Ethan's feet out from under him and pinned him with her sword to his throat.

"Whose side are you on?" Ethan grumbled one afternoon a few days later when Sonia had laid him out flat for the third time.

"Whomever wins," Owen replied with a flirtatious, little smile. Sonia chuckled, giving Owen a quick peck on the cheek.

Ethan's eyes narrowed, and he turned to Sonia again. "Let's play Catch and Fire. Owen hasn't seen it yet."

Sonia raised a brow. "Do you think that's a good idea right now?"

"Of course," Ethan said with a grin. "Why not?"

"What is Catch and Fire?" Owen asked.

"Sonia shoots an arrow at me, and I catch it and fire it back at her through her bow over her head," Ethan said.

That didn't sound particularly fun to Owen, but he was also not a great archer like the Comorran prince and princess. "Come on," Ethan said to Sonia. "Please?"

Sonia glanced over at Owen, then back to Ethan. "All right," she relented. "Just one round."

"All I need," Ethan said, giving Owen a smug grin.

They moved over to the archery field, and Owen took up a place under his usual favorite tree. Sonia tossed Ethan his bow, and he caught it with one hand, giving Owen a glance as he did. Owen smiled shyly at him. Ethan was definitely trying to show off, even more so than usual because Sonia had bested him in sparring.

Sonia picked up an arrow from the quiver, and Owen was relieved to see that the tip of it was not an iron arrowhead but covered in a ball of cotton fabric. Ethan turned his back to her, digging his boots into the loose earth, tensed and ready.

Sonia glanced over at Owen again before lifting the bow. She pulled back the string and exhaled slowly, ruffling the fletching on the end of the arrow, before she called, "Now!" and released the arrow. It flew across the field, and Ethan whirled around, his hand coming up to catch the arrow in midair like he had years ago. He shifted, bringing his own bow up and settling the arrow into it almost faster than Owen could see. However, Owen didn't miss that Ethan shot him a cocky grin before he turned and loosed the arrow back in Sonia's direction. But the grin fell away almost immediately, and Owen could see why before it happened.

Sonia had her bow over her head, Ethan's arrow supposed to go through the gap between the bow and the string, but in his distraction, Ethan had pointed the arrow too low. Sonia turned her face away, which was the only reason the arrow did not break her nose as it struck her in the face. She let out a yell, dropping her bow. In an instant, Owen was on his feet and racing over to her. Ethan looked stunned at his own mistake, his own body slow to move.

Owen pried Sonia's hand from her right cheek. The skin there was already bright red and growing darker by the minute, her eye and cheek starting to swell. He carefully examined her eye, but the arrow seemed to have struck lower, no redness or damage to her eyeball or socket. That was a relief, at least. He glanced up as Ethan came running over, his feet finally responding. "Come on," Owen said to Sonia, taking her by the arm. "Let's get some ice on that right away."

"Sonia, I'm sorry!" Ethan said.

"It's fine," Sonia grumbled, turning away from her brother to follow Owen. Ethan started to trail them, but Sonia gave him a glower. "No," she said sternly, and Ethan fell back. Owen could see the devastation on his face for what he had done, but Sonia was his concern right now.

Owen hurried Sonia to the kitchens to get a compress with ice. Then he and Sonia sat down in her room as she pressed the towel-wrapped ice to her face. "Are you all right?" Owen asked, taking her free hand and rubbing it gently.

"Yes," Sonia said with a sigh. "That's the first time he's missed."

"Really?" Owen asked in surprise.

"Yes, really," Sonia said. "I knew he was distracted with you there, I should have said no."

"I'm sorry," Owen said, squeezing her hand in apology.

"It's not your fault," Sonia soothed, giving Owen's arm a nudge with her shoulder. "I'll just have a black eye for a week or two."

Owen sighed. "I shouldn't have distracted him."

"You didn't do anything," Sonia chided. "He was just trying to show off for you."

"I could tell," Owen said lightly.

"He really does love you," Sonia said.

"He hasn't said it yet," Owen said, meeting Sonia's gaze, hearing his disappointment tumble out with the words.

Sonia stared at him, then let out a huff. "Ugh, of course he hasn't."

"Well, I haven't said it either," Owen said meekly.

"But you do love him."

"I do."

"You might have to say it first," Sonia said, taking the ice off of her puffy eye to examine it with her fingers. "He's an idiot, and you're the romantic."

Owen laughed. "I suppose that's true. But my first priority is making sure he doesn't take out your eye while trying to impress me further."

Sonia snickered and hugged him close. "I make no promises."

Owen hadn't realized how much of a romantic he was from watching his parents, but it made so much sense, especially now that Sonia had told him that Ethan loved him. He wanted Ethan to say it. He wanted to be romanced and swept off his feet and hear the words "I love you." But the words didn't come.

Ethan did not suggest hunting again, which Owen was grateful for, nor did he suggest firing arrows at his sister. He took Owen into town several times, always with Xan or one of the other guards to accompany them, going to pubs where they could play cards with the patrons, or to various stores and markets. When they went out, Ethan would dress in some of his fancier clothes and carry his sword on his belt. He always had a bit of a swagger about him, and he would give Owen a small smirk whenever someone looked enviously at his clothing or his handsome face.

Ethan complimented him a lot too, which Owen appreciated, but he wished that the prince focused less on his outfits and how pretty he was. All of that was superficial and could easily change. They went for walks in the garden together, hand in hand, and Ethan chattered on endlessly, as if trying to fill the silence between them. It might have been romantic if Ethan had asked Owen questions, or even let him get a word in edgewise. Owen tried to quell the nervous chattering from Ethan with kisses and praise, hoping to reassure the dark-haired young man that he didn't need Ethan to impress him, but Ethan's bragging only continued.

He had given Ethan so many chances to say that he loved him, but none of them had panned out, and the summer was rapidly drawing to a close. He was going to have to say it first, just like Sonia had warned him. He had spent the last few weeks in Ethan's room at night, the two of them entwined around each other on the bed, and Owen knew that was where he wanted to be every night. The prince he had given his heart to was there, he just wasn't the romantic that Owen was. That was all right. Owen would open the door instead. His stomach fluttered as he got into the warm bed, Ethan already nestled comfortably in the nest of blankets and pillows.

"Ethan," he said as they curled next to one another.

"Mm." Ethan's voice was no more than an exhalation.

Owen took a deep breath, his heart a drum beat in his chest. "I love you," he whispered in his ear.

"I know."

Owen blinked, staring at Ethan in the darkness. That was not the answer he had expected upon telling Ethan that he loved him. Ethan was supposed to say, 'I love you too,' and hold him close and whisper sweet nothings into his ear. Owen could even do without the sweet nothings part if Ethan had only returned his words. But, 'I know?' What sort of response was that? After nearly the entire summer of waiting, anticipating this moment, to have his words dismissed so easily hurt. Tears burned behind his eyelids, and Owen felt like he might be sick. It hurt even more when he slipped out of the bed, making his way back to his own room to sleep, and Ethan did not even open his eyes when he left.

The next morning, Ethan was as bright and chipper as he could be, while Owen felt like a storm cloud was hovering just over his head. His resentment of Ethan had not melted away with the dawning of the sun. But maybe Ethan had only been tired and would remedy the situation now. Ethan strode into the dining hall with his usual swagger, plopping down into his seat. "Morning."

"Morning," Owen greeted in return. Ethan seemed preoccupied with filling his plate. Owen tried to force some lightness into his tone as he said, "Sleep well?"

"Yeah. Really well," Ethan said. And that was all he said. No declarations of love, no inquiries about how Owen had slept or how he felt today, nothing. Owen felt his stomach clench, suddenly not hungry. "Excuse me," he said, setting his utensils aside and getting up, leaving the room swiftly. He made it back to his own room before the tears fell. He knew Ethan cared about him, but why did it feel like he didn't? They were only days away from leaving for the year, and Owen didn't feel like they had progressed at all beyond that night hunting in the forest when Ethan wasn't sure how to comfort him or talk to him about what happened. A gloom settled over him and stayed there as he prepared to go back to Thornwood with his family, at a loss for what would happen when they left Comorra this time.

Chapter Nine

The morning of the day the royal family was to leave, Owen had butterflies in his stomach, but not good ones. Ethan had looked so excited the night before, casting glances at Owen across the dinner table all evening, but then he had not said anything else before they had gone to their separate beds. He fought down nausea after breakfast, hoping he was wrong about what was about to happen. But as the two courts gathered in the main hall to say their final goodbyes, Ethan grasped his hands, and Owen thought his knees might collapse. "Owen, this summer has been amazing. You're amazing." He lifted Owen's hands, bringing them to his lips to kiss his knuckles. "So, before you go, I want to ask you to marry me."

Owen's breath caught as his fear was made true, his fingers curling in Ethan's hands. "You do?"

"Yes!" Ethan leaned in and tried to kiss him again as the assembled crowd broke into cheers and applause, but Owen pulled back, his cheeks burning with heat.

"Wait."

The room went oddly silent, and Owen suddenly became very aware of all eyes on them. This didn't feel right. He wanted to talk to Ethan, to tell him his feelings, without everyone watching. He turned to Ethan again, trying to keep the desperation out of his voice. "May I speak with you? Alone?"

Ethan blinked in surprise. "I... Yes, of course," he said, motioning to the door that led into the side parlor. Owen turned and headed straight for it, his heart hammering in his ears with each step. Ethan followed after him, closing the door, the silence suddenly deafening. "What is it?"

Owen took a moment to make sure he wasn't going to cry before he turned and met Ethan's gaze. "Why do you love me?"

Ethan stared at him. "What?"

"Why do you love me?" Owen repeated.

"I..." Ethan's cheeks went red, his hands clenching and unclenching as he tried to find words that escaped him. "Because you're wonderful."

"I haven't felt very wonderful with you this year," Owen forced out. There, he had said it. What he knew he should have said weeks, months ago, and he hadn't because the look on Ethan's face now as it crumpled broke his heart.

"Why not?" Ethan asked, reaching out to try to hold him but Owen pulled back.

"Do you not realize how immature you've been this entire summer?"

"What do you mean?" Ethan asked, frowning.

"You've been so selfish," Owen replied. "I love you, and I want to be with you, but you need to think outside of yourself. You need to think about your people and how your actions affect them. And you need to think about me."

"I *do* think about you!" Ethan protested, but Owen cut him off with a wave of his hand.

"Maybe you think you do, but you don't act like it. You don't consider my desires or my safety or my feelings. You're so focused on yourself and showing off. You've spent the entire summer trying to impress me, but you've hardly asked me anything about myself or what I want. It's like I'm one of your servants."

Ethan stared at him in surprise. "You think I treat you like a servant?"

Owen held up his hands in exasperation. "How much do you actually know about me?"

Ethan blinked. "I... what?"

"What's my favorite color?" Owen asked, tipping his head pointedly.

Ethan frowned, seemingly at a loss for words.

"What book am I reading right now?" Owen asked, a bit more force behind his words this time.

"I... don't know," Ethan said, feeling like his tongue weighed a thousand pounds in his mouth.

"When is my birthday?"

"Early spring," Ethan said, confident on that answer, at least.

"But what is the date?"

"Um..." Ethan felt his cheeks flush red.

Owen sighed and shoved his blond hair off his forehead. "Do you love me?"

"Yes!" Ethan declared, loudly and firmly.

Owen's eyes shimmered with tears, and he swallowed hard as a lump formed in his throat. "Do you? Or am I just an amusement? Someone you can show off to who will stroke your ego?"

Ethan stared at him. Where was that coming from? "Owen. Is that all that you think you are to me?"

"I don't know," Owen said, blinking hard as the tears threatened to spill over his lashes. "I want to be more than that."

"You are!" Ethan protested, reaching out to catch his hands, giving them a squeeze. "I want you! You're all I want! I love you!"

Owen swallowed hard, barely able to speak around the lump in his throat now. "You realize that's the first time you've said that the entire summer?"

Ethan blinked. "It... it is?"

Owen nodded. He was losing the battle with his tears, and more than anything, he did not want Ethan to see him cry right now. He swallowed again, but the tightness in his throat refused to go away. "It is."

"I love you!" Ethan said, trying to pull Owen in closer, but Owen stood rigid in place. "I love you, and I don't want anyone but you."

"Then you need to show me." He sniffed and pulled his hands out of Ethan's, immediately missing the warmth of them. "Next summer." That felt like a lifetime from now.

Ethan inhaled sharply. "You can't go," he said, trying to take Owen's hand again, but Owen drew back.

"I have to."

"Stay," Ethan pleaded softly. "Let me prove to you that I love you."

Owen's eyes were deep pools of sapphire blue as he gazed up at him. "You had all summer to do that. I have to leave now." He turned and walked back out the door to where Elistair, Sonia, Stephan, and Amelia all waited. He was sure the crestfallen look on his face was all the answer they needed to know how their conversation went.

Ethan followed him out of the room, his chest so tight he could barely breathe. "Owen..."

Owen shook his head. He didn't want to talk about this further. He knew Ethan loved him, but words were only half of the equation. He needed Ethan to make the effort to mature and know that he meant what he said about loving him. "I'll be back next year," he said softly.

Ethan nodded numbly, reaching up to try to touch Owen's cheek, but Owen pulled away, tears hot and stinging, blurring his vision. "Goodbye, Prince Ethan." And then he turned on his heel and strode away, out the doors of the main hall before anyone else could say anything. He fought back the tears the entire way, only allowing them to fall once he was inside their carriage with the doors closed where no one could see him.

It was silent as his mother and father eventually joined him. Amelia sat next to him and took him gently into her arms. Owen clung to her, sniffling as the tears fell. The carriage began to move, and Owen thought his heart was going to explode in his chest, like a bird trying to break free from its cage. A rumble of thunder overhead mirrored the dark feeling inside of him.

Chapter Ten

He felt like he cried for hours, until he was empty and numb, but finally, Owen pulled his face from Amelia's shoulder. She reached up to stroke the tears from his cheeks as Owen sniffled. She unhooked the cloak from around her shoulders and wrapped it around Owen's own, securing it there, like he was a child crying in his bed. He curled his hands into the soft fabric, recounting the conversation to his parents, as well as Ethan's behavior throughout the summer. Stephan and Amelia listened in silence until he was done and was able to breathe again without tears. "What ails your heart the most, my darling?" Amelia soothed gently.

"Was I too hard on him?" Owen asked softly.

Amelia and Stephan exchanged glances before Stephan gave his son a fond smile. "No, my boy. You both are young, and with youth comes mistakes. But there are still consequences, even if those mistakes were not intentional."

"I know he loves me," Owen said, his voice cracking a little, his cheeks tingling from the tears that still lingered on his skin. "And I do love him. I just want him to show me that he wants me for me."

"It's all right, sweetheart," Amelia soothed, adjusting the cloak around his shoulders. "I know it hurts right now. But it will pass, and you both will come out stronger for it. Every great love has its ups and downs. Learning to navigate when the waters get choppy is an important step in a relationship."

"Indeed," Stephan said, taking Amelia's hand and giving it a squeeze. "Why, when I w-"

The carriage came to a jolting stop, and one of the horses outside let out a whinnying cry. "Whoa," called the driver, trying to steady the nervous horse as the carriage rocked a bit on its wheels.

Amelia frowned, lifting the curtains to try to see the path ahead. "Why have we stopped?"

"I don't know. Stay here," Stephan said. He pushed open the door and stepped out into the cool night. Amelia picked up one of the blankets from the seat, wrapping it around herself and drawing Owen closer.

Ahead on the path stood a dark form, cloak flapping in the wind that rustled through the late summer trees. Stephan stared at the figure as the guards drew in around the carriage protectively. The figure pushed back its hood, and Stephan let out a gasp. "Raric," he said. Inside the carriage, Amelia's head shot up, clenching her fingers around Owen's hand.

No one saw the attack start; three wolves suddenly burst from the trees, growling and snarling, taking down horses and guards alike. Owen heard shouts and screams, the carriage shaking as the horses bridled to it thrashed and tossed. Stephan lost his grip and fell from the doorway. Amelia started toward him, but something impacted the carriage, and everything suddenly pitched wildly to one side. Owen tried to catch Amelia against him to stop her tumbling as the carriage landed on its side with a violent crash.

The door above them was ripped open, and one of the guards extended his hand down to them. "Quickly, my lady," he said. Owen helped Amelia up, giving her a push as best he could at the odd angle and his petite frame, until the guard was able to lift her from the ruined interior. Then the hand extended down to him. Owen had a flash of another strong hand reaching down to help him. He wished just for a moment that Ethan was here. He grasped the guard's hand, giving a little jump to help leverage himself up and out of the prostrated carriage before the guard helped him alight safely on the ground next to Amelia.

The guard turned to them, but something suddenly grabbed him by the back of his cloak and yanked him away with a choked scream. Owen wasn't able to see what happened next in the chaos, but something warm and wet hit his face, and he knew it was not rain. The guard closest to them pointed to the woods. "Run, Your Highnesses!" he said.

Owen grabbed his mother's hand and gave her a pull, stumbling off the path and into the trees. The crash of metal against flesh and shouts festooned the air, and something snapped and growled. Several guards were running with them. One turned back to face whatever was coming their way, and Owen cringed as he heard the man's scream get cut off. Branches snapped, bushes rustled; something was chasing after them. The remaining two guards were between them and their pursuers, but not for long. One was taken out from behind before she could even turn to defend herself, and the last guard landed hard in the mud, something dark on top of him that let out a vicious snarl that Owen could barely hear over the pounding of his own blood in his ears.

Amelia's hand was trembling in his, the dark blanket still clutched around her. Owen saw what he thought was a clearing ahead, tugging her toward it. They battered away a few branches as they emerged from the trees, only to skid to a stop. In front of them, the ground fell away down into a churning river, impossibly high to jump into it. From this height, it would certainly be fatal. Heart pounding in his ears above the rush of the river below, Owen realized they were trapped.

Something large and dark sprang from the forest, catching Amelia in the back, sending her tumbling to the ground, Owen losing his grip on her hand. "Run!" Amelia gasped, lifting her eyes desperately to her son just as a fanged snout wrapped around her throat. The ground beneath her instantly became a puddle of red, and Owen knew he was too late to save her. Tears stung his eyes as Amelia went limp, the monstrous wolf on top of her crushing her tiny body into the mud as it growled, its fiery gaze turning toward Owen. He braced himself for the wolf to spring, but it didn't, just standing and watching him, daring him to move.

He heard the trod of heavy boots approaching, but Owen couldn't pull his eyes away from the wolf. A dark figure emerged from the trees a few steps away, and the wolf backed away from his mother's body to stand next to it. Owen cautiously turned to see a man he did not know. He was an older man, with bushy, red hair peppered with gray that stood out from his craggy cheeks, and dark, glittering eyes that were focused solely on Owen. The man smiled, and maybe it was an attempt at a kind one, but it sent icy chills through him. "Forgive the rough treatment, Your Majesty," the older man crooned in a raspy voice that made Owen think of steel dragged over stone. "I know you are frightened, but I assure you, if you cooperate with me, you have nothing to fear." Behind him, two more wolves, also covered in blood, waited, watching Owen closely. He hoped that they would attack the man in front of him, but they only stood still as the man drew closer and lifted his hand.

Owen braced for a blow, but it did not come. Instead, the man took hold of the hood and pulled it back so it dropped around Owen's shoulders. He stared at the prince as Owen stared back at him, white all around his dark eyes. "You!" he said, falling back a step.

Owen let out a gasp as he realized that the red-haired man must have thought that he was the queen, with his blond hair, fine features, and wrapped as he was in her cloak. "Where is Queen Amelia?" the man demanded.

Owen's eyes unconsciously flickered to the dark blanket and pool of blood nearby. The man followed his gaze, seeming to stiffen. He moved over, lifting the blanket, but Owen couldn't bring himself to look, instead watching the man's reaction.

The man stared in shock for a long moment before his face twisted into a rage that Owen had never seen on anyone before. He dropped the blanket, rising slowly and deliberately to his feet. He looked over at Owen, the fury on his face more frightening than anything Owen had ever seen in his life. The man lifted his gloved hand, and light suddenly arched from his fingertips. It was a strange light, almost like black lightning. Owen braced himself again, but the man suddenly turned away from him. There was a crack, and the smell of something sharp in the air, and then all three of the wolves dropped to the ground, dead eyes staring vacantly at nothing.

Owen gasped as the name his father had spoken came back to him. He had only ever heard of one man who could kill with magic, and he had thought that man to be long departed from their lives. "Raric," he breathed, his heart hammering in his chest as his knees went weak.

Raric's face burned with cold fury as he stalked over to Owen. His leather-clad hand reached up to grip Owen's chin and lift it, and Owen could see the deep lines etched around the man's eyes and over his cheeks. Wherever Raric had been all of these years, life had not been kind to him. "Well, well. It looks like today is your lucky day, little prince," Raric said, and his thumb brushed over Owen's lower lip.

"Wh... what do you want?" Owen asked, not sure if his words carried over the thunder of his heart and the rain and wind around them, despite Raric being so close to him.

"We'll discuss that, Your Highness, but not here." The next moment, his body sagged into black-clad arms as involuntary darkness came over him.

Chapter Eleven

When he came to again, Owen found himself straddling a horse. There was something over his head that he assumed was a burlap bag, scratchy and damp from rain. Someone was pressed close up behind him, so close that Owen could smell the leather of the man's tunic even through the bag. His hands were trapped in front of him, tied together at the wrists, so he simply balled them into fists and willed himself not to cry. He wanted to pull away from Raric, but there was nowhere for him to go. Without being able to see what was around him or being able to brace his fall, throwing himself from a horse at full canter did not seem like a wise idea. He was unsure how much time had passed, but he was sure it had been hours by the way his stomach tightened with hunger. He gripped the horse as best he could with his legs, and though the touch revulsed him, Raric's arms around him kept him firmly in place.

The world beyond the sack that still encompassed his head was brighter when they finally stopped. The whole night must have passed. He gave a squirm as the horse slowed to a walk, and Raric's deep chuckle sounded in his ear. "Almost there, little princeling."

Owen's heart raced as he wondered where 'there' was. They had ridden through the night but had not boarded a ship or a wagon. They had to still be in Comorra, or perhaps, beyond one of its borders in The Wilds that surrounded it where it did not meet the Sapphire Sea. That thought made his pinching stomach twist with fear.

The horse stopped a few minutes later, and Raric slid down, groaning and stretching before his hands reached up and caught Owen's hips, lifting him down with surprising gentleness. Owen's feet slid until he found his footing, little-used muscles in his legs burning from the long ride. The bag was suddenly yanked off of his head, morning sunlight blinding him and making him squeeze his eyes shut. He inhaled the cool air and smelled water and forest and horse.

"There is nowhere to run, Your Highness," Raric said, and Owen's heart skipped a beat when he heard the sound of a dagger being unsheathed from a belt, his eyes flying open again. He tried to backpedal, but his feet caught on the slick ground, and he would have fallen if Raric had not grabbed him and hauled him upright again. He took one of the prince's bound hands and jabbed the tip of the blade into the heel of Owen's palm. Owen let out a cry of pain. A moment later, the ties holding his wrist were cut, giving instant relief to his shoulders. He clutched his bleeding palm with his other hand, curling it protectively to his chest as he looked up at Raric.

The man held a large silver locket on a heavy chain, with some sort of runes carved into it that Owen could not see clearly. Raric tipped his dagger, and a drop of Owen's blood dripped off the sharp tip to fall into the open locket. Raric snapped the locket closed with a sharp click before tucking the dagger securely back into his belt.

"Where are we?" Owen demanded, glancing around as he brushed his damp, blond hair off his forehead with his non-bleeding hand.

He and Raric were standing at the edge of a lake that surrounded the ruins of what might have once been a monastery or a small castle. One of its walls had caved in, and most of its windows were broken.

Raric ignored the question, slipping the locket around his neck and tucking it securely into his shirt. Owen watched that with a mounting sense of dread. He knew little of magic, and even less of black magic, but he was sure a sorcerer having his blood was not something to be trifled with.

"Now, little prince, let us talk business. Man to man, as it were." Raric gestured to a log nearby. "Sit."

"I'll stand, thank you," Owen said bitterly.

Raric shrugged. "Suit yourself. You have your mother's spirit, that's for sure."

"And you killed her," Owen said, the words sticking in his throat.

Raric snorted, his face twisting into a dark scowl. "An unfortunate accident. Didn't think those creatures would be so stupid. You were wearing her cloak, of course. I should have been more cautious. Ah well." He waved his hand. "What's done is done."

"What is it that you want?" Owen asked, narrowing his eyes, not wanting to hear Raric speak about his mother anymore.

"It's quite simple," Raric said with a dark grin. "I want you to marry me."

Owen's stomach flipped inside of him, and he took a step back on the squishy bank. "What?"

"Never much been into men," Raric said thoughtfully, looking him up and down with a gaze that made Owen feel like he was stripped bare. "But you are quite pretty. Just like your mother was. You really do look so much alike."

"Why would you want me to marry you?" Owen demanded.

Raric chuckled that harsh, grating laugh of his. "Don't mistake my intentions, Your Highness. I don't want you. What I want is your father's kingdom."

"Take it then," Owen said with a glower. "If I'm your prisoner, I can't do much to stop you."

"Nah." Raric waved his hand as if brushing the idea away like a pesky fly. "You see, little prince, if you take something that isn't yours, you spend the rest of your life trying to defend it from others who would take it from you." His lips curved into a devious smile. "But, if you gave me a place at your side, as Stephan's only heir, why, no one could dismiss that, could they?"

Owen felt ice prickle in his stomach. If he took Raric as his spouse, Raric would be the next in line for the throne, and then Owen was sure it would only be a matter of time before he outlived his usefulness to him and ended up like his parents. "Was that your plan when you attacked us? You would kill my father and I and then convince my mother to marry you?"

Raric laughed. "I knew it would be a challenge, but eventually the queen would see sense."

Owen snarled darkly. "She would never, and neither will I!"

Raric's chuckle was deeper still. "So determined, little princeling. But don't worry. I have all the time in the world to wait for you to come around."

Raric reached into his shirt to pull the locket out. One hand closed around it as he raised his other hand, and Owen suddenly felt like he was trapped in a windstorm that swirled in all directions, pulling at his hair and his clothes. Dizziness hit him, and he squeezed his eyes shut as the world suddenly dropped.

When he opened them again, Raric still stood before him, but he was suddenly much taller than he had been only moments before. Something tingled inside Owen's chest, like insects buzzing deep within him, and the breeze around him made his skin prickle. He glanced down, only to find himself staring at a pair of orange, webbed feet. Everything suddenly felt off, and he staggered. He turned toward the water, then pulled up short at the reflection staring back at him. A white, long-necked swan gazed back in confusion from the surface of the lake. He reached out a hand to touch the water, as if it were merely an illusion, then recoiled in shock as the hand he reached out was not a hand at all, but a long wing covered with pointed, white feathers. A cry escaped his lips, and he could hear that the sound was not his own voice, but a loud, bird-like screech.

"Now, calm down, Your Highness," Raric said, reaching out a hand and putting it on the top of Owen's head. Owen snapped at him with what he realized was a curved, orange beak. Raric pulled his hand back with a smirk. "You do have fight in you. But that's all right. I can be just as stubborn as you."

Owen hissed, trying to form words, but all that came out was a ridiculous honking sound, and he closed his mouth, glaring at Raric instead.

"Now, don't let my little spell get you down," Raric said. "It's only temporary. Every night, when the moonlight touches your wings, you'll turn back into a human. You have to be on the lake, of course, so don't get any foolish notions of running off."

Owen glowered darkly. Raric smirked. "All it takes for me to lift the spell is for you to marry me. I can be a patient man, Owen."

Owen hissed at him again, and Raric laughed. "I will return tonight to see if you've changed your mind. Good day, Your Highness." He turned on his heel and disappeared into the woods, leaving Owen alone at the edge of the lake.

Chapter Twelve

The day grew hot, and Owen eventually realized he needed to take care of himself. He drank from the lake, and, after a little trial and error, found that he could dive under the water. There were fish in the lake, and it took him the better part of the day to figure out how to catch them in his new swan form, but eventually he did. He nibbled on some of the plants around the shore too. At least his taste buds seemed to have adapted to being a swan as well, which he was oddly grateful for.

He drifted on the lake for a long while, alone with his thoughts, then took a nap in the shade when the heat became too much. His mother was dead, and likely his father as well. Perhaps the ship to take them back to Thornwood would realize something was wrong when the royal carriage had not shown up late that night or early that morning to travel home. But then what? He imagined a messenger would be dispatched to Monarch Elistair's castle to see if perhaps the king and queen had been delayed. Maybe the wreckage of their carriage would be discovered along the way. Would anyone notice that he was not amongst the bodies? Would they think to look for him? But even if they did, how would they know where to even start? He had no idea where he was himself.

His heart sank when he thought about Ethan. His not-quite-yet-fiancé would hear the news of the attack, and he would not know if Owen was alive or dead. At least if he were dead amongst the wreckage, Ethan would be spared the pain of not knowing. He wanted to see the dark-haired prince so badly right now. Ethan would hold him while he grieved, would stroke his hair and whisper words of comfort to him. Silent tears fell from his eyes onto his downy, white chest as he waited for night to arrive.

The royal carriage had not arrived at the port as scheduled. As noon approached with no word from the missing retinue, crew from the Thornwood ship were dispatched to see if things had been delayed. Halfway through the woods, they found the shattered carriage and a scene of carnage. Horses and soldiers lay scattered about, King Stephan amongst them. Queen Amelia and several of the guards were also found in the trees not far away. One of the sailors immediately rode along the forest path, through the town, to the castle. "Murder!" he shouted as he approached the castle gates. "King Stephan is dead!"

The gates were thrown wide, and the man was ushered to where Elistair had been meeting with some of the other nobles, both

Ethan and Sonia by their side. The man dropped into a hasty bow, breathing hard as he forced out, "King Stephan and Queen Amelia. They are dead, Your Majesty. Their carriage was found wrecked in the woods. The soldiers are all dead as well."

Before Elistair could speak, Ethan shot to his feet. "What about Prince Owen?" he demanded.

The sailor shook his head. "He had not been found when I came here, Your Highness," he said. The words had not even fully left his mouth before Ethan was sprinting out of the room, through the main hall, and outside. He grabbed the first horse he saw, which happened to be the one the sailor had arrived on, and gave it a ferocious kick to get it moving. The horse whinnied and dashed back down the path it had just come. Ethan's heart was in his throat. King Stephan and Queen Amelia dead. It did not seem possible; he had only seen them off yesterday.

He saw the wreckage ahead and pulled the horse to a stop. The crew there had gathered the bodies, and Ethan leaped down to frantically search between them. His heart dropped when he saw white-blond hair, but further inspection showed him that it was Queen Amelia. Her head had nearly been severed from her body by what looked like an animal attack. He looked around again, but there were no more bodies with hair that color. He turned to the nearest sailor. "Where is Prince Owen?" he demanded.

The sailor looked at him with worried eyes. "We have not found him, Your Highness," she said. "We have someone dispatched to the ship to bring more people to help search the woods."

"What did this?" Ethan asked, looking around at the violent scene. Blood spattered the ground and the trees. The carriage had been tipped over and had claw marks all over the sides of it, as if from some sort of great animal.

"We found three wolves dead nearby," one of the other crew said despairingly.

Wolves wouldn't normally attack like this, Ethan thought. Even a pack of wolves or a group of bears would not go after a caravan in such a manner, especially when many of those people were trained and armored soldiers.

"Your Highness," someone said, and Ethan turned to see one of the crew pointing at a large burn mark on the outside of the carriage. He moved over to study it. The wood was scorched and blackened, but there were no signs of fire. No bodies were charred or burned either. The sailor studied it with unease. "I've never seen a burn like this before."

"Magic." The word left Ethan's mouth before he had time to think about it, and his heart plummeted into his stomach. If they were dealing with a magic user, he didn't even want to think about what terrible fate might have befallen Owen. He wanted to scream and cry, but he could do that later when he was alone. Right now, he needed to find who did this to the royal family of Thornwood, and he needed to find Owen.

Chapter Thirteen

The sun began to set, casting the sky into the most beautiful rainbow of colors, fading to an ombre of dark purple. Owen stayed near the lake. If Raric's words were true, and the magic only worked if he was on the lake when the moon touched it, he did not want to stray too far. He also felt incredibly vulnerable in this form. Surely in the woods were all manner of beasts or hunters who would love to make a meal of a swan. His mind drifted back to the hunting trip Ethan had taken him on and how easily Ethan had dispatched the various animals. There was no differentiating himself from them now.

It felt like it took forever for the sun to fully set and the moon to rise. Owen didn't think he had ever watched the sky so closely as he did tonight. But sure enough, when the moon rose and spilled its light over the lake's glassy surface, streaming over his angelic-white feathers, he felt the wind rush around him. The dizziness hit him again, and he closed his eyes, feeling mist from swirls of water lightly touch his cheeks and eyelashes. And then, as quickly as it had come, it subsided. Owen opened his eyes and immediately saw that he was standing on human legs again, his leather boots in almost knee-deep water. His own rippling reflection looked back at him, and he breathed a sigh of relief. He turned and strode out of the lake, glad that his boots were at least good quality and did not leak. He was miserable enough without soggy feet. He sat down on the edge of the bank, trying to decide what his next move would be.

He debated running now, but he had no idea where he might go. Without a horse, he might run all night through the forest and never find civilization, only to return to his swan form at daybreak. He supposed he could explore the forest. Certainly, Raric would be living somewhere, either inside of the abandoned monastery or in some sort of camp in the woods. If he found him, he might find his horse, and perhaps a map that would give him an idea of where he was. But he also didn't know if Raric had other creatures guarding the area, as he had controlled the wolves to attack their caravan.

Something rustled in the bushes nearby, and Owen's head shot up, heart hammering. "Who's there?" he asked.

Something poked out of the underbrush a few feet away. It was a tiny face, with round, dark eyes, and a whiskery muzzle. Owen gasped, and the face cocked curiously to the side. Owen held out his hand toward it. "It's all right. I won't hurt you."

The face hesitated again, and then a long body emerged from the leaves, the moonlight catching thick, coarse fur and feet with webbing between each of the dark toes. The creature stood up on its short, hind legs, and Owen smiled when he recognized it to be a species of otter. "Hello," he greeted.

The otter regarded him for another moment before it held out one webbed front foot. "Hello," it said.

Owen cautiously reached out, taking the surprisingly large paw in his own hand and giving it a gentle shake. "My name is Owen."

The otter blinked, then giggled, whiskers twitching. "I'm Amaryllis."

"I'm pleased to meet you, Miss Amaryllis," Owen said, giving her a polite bow of his head, feeling a little improper for sitting on the ground while doing so, but he was at least at her height this way.

The otter shook her head. "My friends call me Alli. You can call me Alli too, Owen."

"Very well," Owen said congenially, rather delighted that Alli already considered him a friend.

Alli smiled, then glanced over her shoulder at the bushes. "It's all right," she called. Nothing moved. Alli frowned, dropping to all fours. "You can come out." Again, nothing happened, save for the wind blowing. Alli frowned. "I'll be right back." She suddenly dashed into the bushes faster than Owen could see. There was a muffled conversation, followed by an indignant yelp, and Alli came bounding back out of the bush with something in her mouth. She skidded to a stop in front of Owen, and he could see that it was a black and yellow salamander, clutched lightly between her jaws as it flailed and shouted. Alli dropped the salamander onto the dirt and put a paw on its back to keep it from running.

"Unhand me, vile beast!" the salamander shouted, its tiny legs waving in the air from under Alli's foot.

"You're being rude," Alli said, and the salamander went still, staring up at Owen from down on the ground. "Owen, this is Willie."

The salamander let out a huff. "That is SIR William Farthington to you!"

Alli rolled her eyes but let the small creature up from the ground. "He thinks he's a knight."

"I *am*!" Sir William declared, pushing himself up on his stumpy hind legs to brush mud from his spotted tummy. He gave Owen a once-over glance up and down. "And you are?"

Owen chuckled. "I'm Owen. Prince of Thornwood."

Sir William blinked his dark eyes at him, then suddenly dropped into an awkward one-knee bow. "Your Highness!" he gasped, reaching out and taking Owen's hand. He pressed a kiss to it, which was strange, since Owen didn't think salamanders had lips. "Please forgive my rudeness. We are honored to be in your presence!" He glanced over at Alli out of the corner of his eye and glowered. "Show His Highness some respect!"

Alli looked confused. "Prince of Thornwood? You mean, the kingdom across the sea?"

Owen nodded slowly. "Yes. My father is King Stephan. I mean..." A painful lump formed in Owen's throat, followed suddenly by hot tears behind his eyes. "I mean, he was. And my mother was Queen Amelia."

"What do you mean, 'was?'" Alli asked.

"They're dead," Owen said softly. "Raric attacked us and killed them. My mother, at least, but probably my father too."

Alli and Sir William both stared at him, stunned, for a moment, before Sir William let out a tiny snarl, his thick tail lashing like a cat about to pounce. "How dare he! I will thrash that coward within an inch of his life!"

Alli's foot came down on Sir William again to hold him in place. "That's horrible," she said softly. "Are you all right?"

Owen let out a sniff. "I... I don't know. I don't know what's happening."

Alli quickly hurried over and climbed onto Owen's lap, smooshing Sir William further into the dirt as she did. "It's okay," she said, taking Owen's cheeks gently in her paws. "We're here for you now."

Owen smiled weakly, reaching up a hand to scratch lightly behind Alli's ear. "Thank you," he said. Alli's fur was thick and warm and comforting. "Do you live here?"

Alli nodded. "All my life. Willie has been here for a while now too." Sir William huffed in agitated agreement.

"Where are you from?" Owen asked the little salamander curiously.

"I was a knight to your father, King Stephan," Sir William said. "A few years ago, His Majesty did not receive the usual letter from Ubertlund, so he tasked me with traveling there and finding what had happened to Raric. I found the outpost there in ruins, and the soldiers there dead or missing. It took me a long time to track Raric down after that. But I found him."

"And the wizard wasn't too happy about it," Alli said dramatically. "So, he turned him into a newt."

"At least you're alive," Owen said, trying to be positive about it.

Sir William sighed. "Indeed. I am sorry I was unable to fulfill my duty to your father, Your Highness."

"But you did," Owen said firmly. "You found Raric, and because of you, we know he is capable of turning humans into animals."

Sir William looked uncertain, but he nodded. "I suppose that is true. But I am still sorry that I was captured and unable to report back to your father to warn him, Your Highness."

"Why did the wizard leave you alive?" Alli asked, settling onto Owen's lap comfortingly.

"He meant to capture my mother instead of me," Owen said, stroking over Alli's head. "To try to force her into marriage."

"You have always looked like your mother," Sir William said, his voice kind. "She was a wonderful woman. I hope she and your father are at peace."

Owen nodded, a few tears gliding silently down his cheeks. Alli reached up to brush them gently away with her webbed feet. "We're here for you, Owen. We're going to help you get away. Right, Willie?"

Sir William nodded. "Indeed we shall! Never fear, Your Highness, we shall defend you with our lives!"

Owen smiled at that. "Thank you."

Alli opened her mouth to say something, but the sound of footsteps approaching from the woods caused her head to shoot up, and she leaped from Owen's lap into the water. Sir William scuttled away to hide behind a rock at the water's edge just as Raric stepped from the tree line.

"Good evening, little prince," he said with a mock bow.

Owen scrambled to his feet, glowering at the magician. "What do you want?"

Raric chuckled. "I see your day on the lake has not dampened your spirit."

"I told you, I'll die before I marry you," Owen said.

Raric made a soft sound in his throat, reaching up to try to take Owen's chin in his hand, but Owen smacked his fingers away. "If you say so, Your Highness. My spell on you will still be in effect if I die before it is removed. So, you do only have limited time to consider my offer. I suggest you keep that in mind." Then he turned and disappeared into the trees once more.

Alli and Sir William emerged out of their hiding places, and Alli rubbed her wet cheek sympathetically on Owen's hand. "Don't worry. We're going to protect you."

"Thank you," Owen said gratefully. If he had friends to talk to and support him, he would be able to hold out against Raric's demand, for as long as it took to find his way out of this terrible situation.

Chapter Fourteen

The lake was not overly large, but the island in the center where the abandoned monastery sat was not easy to reach as a human. Owen had first thought it to be empty, but the next evening, after Raric came to ask him the same question about marriage, instead of leaving into the trees, he had muttered a spell under his breath and conjured a small single-person boat to row himself across the lake to the island. As soon as he stepped out of the boat, it vanished again, and Raric stalked up into the ruins. A few moments later, light flickered and glowed inside, as if Raric had lit a torch and was moving through the building. And there he stayed, the rest of the night, and the entire next day.

When Owen turned back into a swan at daybreak, he swam over to the island, waddling up onto the shore to examine it. The ruins were bigger than they had appeared from the bank. It was a large building, though not as large as the castle in Comorra. He didn't dare explore the structure with Raric inside of it. He had no idea what Raric might decide to do while he was in his vulnerable swan form, so he decided staying away from him was the best choice for now.

"There has to be a way to break the spell, right?" Alli mused thoughtfully as they all sat on the riverbank that afternoon. "All spells must be able to be reversed."

That seemed logical, though Owen's knowledge of magic was fairly limited. "That sounds like it could be true."

Alli stroked her whiskers for a moment, then suddenly gave an excited hop. "I've got it, I've got it!" She pointed one clawed front foot toward the crumbling structure. "If that's where the wizard keeps his magic stuff, maybe there will be a book in there about magic and how to break curses!"

Owen beamed at her. "It's worth trying!" he said eagerly. Raric was at the ruins now, so going tonight was out of the question. He might be willing to risk himself, but he would not put Alli and Sir William in danger if he could avoid it. If they couldn't find any information, at least they would be in the same position they were in now.

Raric did not come to him that night, nor did he appear the next day while Owen flew awkwardly around the lake area, testing out his wings. He debated trying to fly through the woods, which would be faster than running, but he had no idea which direction to go, and there was the ever-present threat of hunters, especially this time of year as the weather began to grow cold and many animals migrated or prepared to hibernate.

That night, Owen was on pins and needles waiting for Raric in the hopes that he would leave into the forest. When he finally emerged from the ruins, Owen had to force himself to not bounce with impatience, instead glowering at the older man as he approached on his magical boat. "Well, now, my little captive prince. I am guessing from that sour look that you still have not changed your mind," Raric said as he stepped from the craft that vanished once more.

"Do you really think I would marry you after what you did to my family?" Owen asked with a dark glare.

"Casualties of war, I'm afraid," Raric said with a shrug, as if killing a dozen people was an everyday occurrence for him.

"This isn't a war," Owen snapped.

"Not yet," Raric said with a cold grin. "You've never seen a war, little prince. The bloodshed, the suffering. The screams of the women and children, the cries of pain and torment." He waved his hand, and the air around them trembled and seemed to melt into a blazing inferno of a battlefield. The crash of horses and riders, steel on steel, was nearly deafening. In the distance, he could see a village on fire, smoke rising thick from the roofs. Soldiers he did not recognize were dragging people from inside the burning huts and slaughtering them with axes and swords. Blood stained the dirt a muddy red. Owen watched in horror as one of the soldiers grabbed a young woman by her hair and forced her to the ground, tearing at her dress.

"Stop it!" he said, clapping his hands to his ears and squeezing his eyes shut to try to block out the carnage around him. "Stop!" His knees buckled, and he landed on the bank, a sob wracking his whole body.

And suddenly, the illusion was gone, replaced once more by the silent night. Raric smirked down at him as Owen slowly let go of his ears, tears stinging his face. "War is terrible, little prince. But so easy to avoid. One little word from you is all it takes."

"Never," Owen snarled.

Raric's face darkened. "Very well. It looks like you need another day to think about it." He turned with a swish of his cloak and stalked into the trees.

Owen wasn't even sure if Raric was out of earshot before Sir William and Alli came bounding out of the bushes. "What a horrid villain!" Sir William declared. "Come back and fight like a man, you coward! I shall tear off your ears and have them fried in duck fat!" He lashed his tail and waved his tiny fists in front of him like a boxer.

Alli moved over to nuzzle against Owen's ankles. "Are you all right, Owen?"

Owen nodded slowly, quickly brushing tears away with a damp sleeve. "Yes," he said firmly before reaching down to pick up Sir William. The salamander huffed in Raric's direction.

"I will relish the day we are able to show that sorcerer that he has messed with the wrong men!"

"Hopefully we can find a way to break the spell on you too," Owen said.

Sir William gave him a delighted grin. "I would be ever so grateful, Your Highness."

"You're not under any spells, are you, Alli?" Owen asked the otter as she nuzzled around his ankles.

"I don't think so. I'm happy being an otter," Alli replied with a toothy smile.

Owen glanced at the ruins of the castle, then at where Raric had disappeared. The lake was too deep for him to walk to the monastery, and the distance was too great to swim. He was sure he would not be able to make it all the way in his human form, so they were going to have to wait until daybreak. He kept watch until the sun came up and he transformed again, but Raric did not return.

Once the sun rose, Sir William sat on Owen's silky, white back as Owen and Alli paddled across the lake to the ruins. With a final glance back at the forest, where nothing moved apart from the leaves, they climbed up the stairs and inside the crumbling structure.

It was not as dilapidated on the inside as the outside. The steps were overgrown with vines and weeds, but they were still solid under their feet. "Where do we look first?" Alli asked as they moved inside, faint beams of sunlight streaming down through the missing chunks of roof.

"The tower," Owen said, nodding his gangly neck upward. "That's where I see his light most of the time."

Alli nodded and turned to scamper up the stairs, avoiding bits of rubble. Owen gave his wings a little flap. He was still not entirely used to flying, and having Sir William on his back did not help his balance, but he managed to follow Alli up the stairs to a second level, and then a third. There was a heavy, wooden door closed at the end of the hallway, and Alli headed toward it. "I bet that's the tower door!"

Owen followed after her, landing on the ground and staring up at the door handle. He didn't have thumbs, he realized, so this was going to be difficult. "Gimme a boost," Alli said, scrambling up onto his back and sending Sir William tumbling to the floor with a splutter. Owen pushed his back end up as high as he could go, and

Alli reached up her paws to grasp the heavy, silver knob. She gave it a twist, then frowned and tried again before she let out a sigh. "It's locked."

Owen looked around for a key, but he saw nothing nearby. "Raric must have the key," he said with a groan.

Alli glanced thoughtfully at the small gap between the door and the floor before her dark eyes lit up with delight. She snatched up Sir William and shoved him face-first under the space. "Get in there and unlock it from the other side."

"Unhand me, peasant!" Sir William sputtered, but Alli only shoved him harder.

"Come on, you can do it."

Sir William swatted her with his tail. "All right, all right, let me go." Alli released him, and Sir William flattened himself almost fully to the ground, shimmying carefully under the door. About halfway in, he got stuck, his tail wriggling as his toes scraped at the stone floor, trying to find purchase. Then, with a rather ungraceful-sounding noise, he disappeared under the jamb.

Everything was quiet for a long moment. Alli peered under the crack of the door. "Willie!" she whispered loudly.

"Hold your horses, I do not see you doing the climbing here," Sir William said from behind the door. There was silence again, and then the door clicked. Owen gave Alli another boost, and she twisted the knob, the door creaking open. Sir William was perched on the doorframe, having climbed it like a tree to the lock on the inside. "Haha!" he cried, jumping down onto Owen's back again and pointing at the twisting stairwell they had found. "No lock shall defeat us! Onward!"

Alli hurried up the dark steps, and Owen flapped his wings to follow. The passage was narrow, and it took a little while for them to safely reach the top. But when they did, the staircase opened up into a large circular room with a single solid window.

Weapons, strange looking glass jars full of things he could not identify, cauldrons, books, and papers were everywhere. Obviously, this was where Raric kept most of his spell crafting and magic items. Nearly everything in this room had once been banned because of its use in dark magic.

"What do we look for?" Alli asked, glancing around the room with concern.

"He has a silver locket with my blood in it," Owen said. "And let's look at the books and papers." He was not about to mess with the jars and potions. Sir William scuttled off his back and up one of the bookshelves, starting to peruse the titles. Alli climbed up onto a nearby plinth, and Owen perched on the edge of a table where several books lay open. He started to page through them. There were spells for everything, from the mundane to the absolutely grotesque. Some of the spells had drawings next to them, portrayals of what they could do, or runes written in a language he did not understand. He hoped that the information they sought would be something they would be able to read.

The first book held nothing useful for his situation, so Owen carefully replaced it back where it had been before moving on to the next one. This seemed to be mostly about herbs and poisons. Owen shuddered to himself. He was almost glad that his mother was not there. The thought of Raric doing something cruel to her with his magic made his stomach roil inside of him. He moved on to the third book. He flipped a few pages before realizing with a gasp of delight that it was a book on animal transmutation. Within a few more pages, he had found a drawing of a salamander that looked nearly identical to Sir William. "Does this sound familiar?" he asked the newt. Sir William scuttled over to him, perching on Owen's head to peer down at the book.

"Yes, I do believe that incantation is the one he used, and I distinctly remember the scent of rosemary, which is indicated in the elements. This must be the one! Wonderful work, Your Highness!" Sir William crowed in delight.

Owen gave an excited little hop before scanning to the bottom of the page where the antidotes and reversals to the spells were listed. "The spell may be reversed with a kiss from a virgin," Owen said.

"Ah-hah!" Sir William said triumphantly. "That should be simple enough! Your Highness, would you be so kind?"

"Oh, I'm not-" Owen started.

"Willie!" Alli cut in sharply. "You can't ask Owen to kiss you when we don't know what might affect his own spell."

Sir William blushed a strange red color. "Ah, you are right. Forgive me, Your Highness, I was momentarily overcome. Let us find the reversal for your curse." He slid down Owen's neck and onto the table.

Owen flipped a few more pages. He found information on how to turn one's self into various creatures and even into other people. He could see why dark magic had been banned; there was so much damage that could be done with a relatively simple spell. Another page turn, and a beautiful sketch of a swan met his gaze. "Here!" he said eagerly, starting to read, and Sir William stood on his hind legs to read along. Alli shimmied down the plinth and up the table leg to join them.

"The spell has two parts," Owen said with a groan. "Transforming into a swan during the day, and returning to human form at night. The one who is cursed must be kissed by their one true love, and then their one true love must prove their eternal love in word and deed."

"That is... very open-ended," Alli said.

"At least mine is a simple smooch," Sir William agreed.

"Why is yours so much more difficult?" Alli said with a dramatic whine, draping her head backwards off the table.

Owen sighed, his own head drooping a little. "I suppose the fact that I become human again makes it more complex than what happened to Sir William."

Sir William gave Owen's webbed foot a gentle pat with his tiny foot. "Do you have a true love?"

"I do," Owen said, perking up a bit. "My... um... I suppose he is almost my fiancé, Prince Ethan of Comorra!"

Alli squealed and clapped her paws. "Oh, that's adorable! I want to meet him! When's the wedding?"

Owen laughed brightly. "Next summer, hopefully." He wondered if he would ever see Ethan again. "How far are we from Comorra?"

"I believe we are just outside of it," Sir William said, pushing aside a precarious stack of papers to show a large map unrolled underneath them. "When I found the fiend, I had only just crossed the border into The Wilds. Ah, here!" he said, pointing one tiny toe at a dotted line demarcating the edge of Comorra. "So, we must be here." He pointed to a blue spot on the map with a small, green island in the center of it. There was a label next to it, but it had been scratched out with ink, so the name was no longer visible.

Owen traced the tip of his wing over the map. "The castle where Monarch Elistair and Ethan and Sonia live is here," he said, indicating the large structure. He sighed dejectedly. "It's too far for me to run in a single night. And if I'm not on the lake when the moon rises, I won't transform into a human again. Ethan wouldn't recognize me as a swan."

Alli hummed thoughtfully. "So, we need to bring Ethan to you."

"How would we do that?" Sir William said with a huff. "It's not like we can simply write a note for him to come find you."

"A note!" Alli and Owen said at the same time. Owen glanced around the room, finding a loose piece of parchment.

"If I write a note to Ethan, could you get it to the castle? Or at least to somewhere it will be found and delivered to him?" Owen asked eagerly.

Alli nodded, her dark eyes bright. "Yes! Let's do it!"

Owen looked around for a quill and ink, but there seemed to be nothing. Perhaps Raric had anticipated that Owen might try to send a note for help. But he was a swan. A quill was easily remedied.

They crossed over the lake to the shore again, the parchment rolled and held carefully in Owen's beak to keep it dry. Once they reached the bank, he found a spot in a hollow log to store it, then turned to Alli. "Pull out one of my tail feathers so I have something to write with."

Alli spat into her palms and rubbed them together before grabbing one of Owen's tail feathers. "Ready?"

"Ready." Owen closed his eyes, bracing his webbed feet into the mud.

"One. Two. Three." Alli yanked hard, and Owen yelped, tears stinging his eyes as the feather came free, along with a drop of blood at the tip. Alli gave his tail a soothing pat. "I'm sorry."

"It's all right," Owen replied, sniffling and taking a deep breath. It hurt, but the pain was already lessening, and he would yank out every feather on his body if it meant that he would escape from Raric. And then there was nothing to do but wait for the sun to go down.

As soon as he transformed into a human, Owen grabbed the parchment and the tail feather. There was plenty of mud on the shore. But between the mud easily smearing and the quill not having a proper carved tip, it was slow going. He also was keeping his eyes and ears open in case Raric returned. The letter was not elegant, but it was legible, and that was what was important. He wrote everything he could think of, with his location, the details of the curse and how to lift it, and letting Ethan know about Raric and his dangerous magic.

Once it was finished, he did his best to dry it with his breath and the wind, not wanting to roll it or fold it before it was fully dry so the mud would not smear. Raric still had not appeared, and Owen was wondering if perhaps he might not come at all as dawn approached.

He had just folded the letter to give to Alli when he heard boots approaching through the trees. Owen quickly shoved both the letter and the feather into his shirt, patting it into place as best he could. A moment later, Raric stepped out of the forest, giving him a cold smile.

"Hello, Owen."

Owen just glared at him.

Raric sighed dramatically. "Oh, you're not speaking to me now?"

"I have nothing to say to you," Owen growled.

"What is it that turns you from me, little prince?" Raric asked. "It's true, I am not a young man. But if that would help." Raric lifted his hand and swiped it over his own face. Black lightning crackled, and suddenly the pitted, lined face of Raric was gone. In its place was a youth around Owen's age, strong-jawed and handsome, with red hair cut short and curled over a smooth forehead. Owen's breath caught at the unexpected look.

Raric smiled, though it was a cold smile that did not reach his dark eyes. "Is this what you want, Your Highness? Someone young and handsome? I can maintain this look when we are together, and I promise, you will never want for other company in your bed."

Owen thought he might throw up. He reached up and slapped Raric across the cheek. In an instant, the handsome mask was gone, and Raric glowered at him from his world-worn face. "You are a monster, no matter what form you take," Owen hissed. "I would rather die than marry you."

Raric let out a snarl of anger, a bright mark on his cheek from Owen's palm. "You want to continue to try my patience, boy? Very well." He gave Owen a shove, and Owen fell backward into the lake hard on his backside, water instantly soaking his pants and the sleeves of his shirt. Raric stared coldly down at him. "You can keep denying me, Owen, but one day soon, I'm going to boil over."

"And then what?" Owen asked, getting to his feet despite the ache in his spine from his landing. "You'll kill me?"

Raric smirked at that, reaching out to touch Owen's cheek. "Oh no, Your Highness. I wouldn't just kill you. If I have reason to turn my wrath on you, I'll make sure you suffer for it."

Owen shuddered and pulled away from the hand on his face. "One day, I will get away from you," he said, glaring at the magician.

"You're welcome to try," Raric said. "Of course, you'll have to do it without these." He grabbed Owen by the front of his shirt and shoved his hand inside, snatching out the folded parchment and quill. Owen went pale as Raric threw back his head and laughed. "You are quite the resourceful one, little princeling, I'll give you that." There was a sizzle of black flame, and the letter and quill burned in a flash in his hand. Owen felt his heart break in his chest as the letter to Ethan fluttered to the ground, nothing more than ash. "I'm willing to forgive this little indiscretion of yours. What do you say?"

Owen clenched his fists at his side. "I don't care what you do to me. I will never let you have my family's kingdom."

"It seems you need another day to think about it." Raric waved his hand at the sky. Owen's throat tightened as he turned to see the sun just beginning to break over the horizon. The next moment, the wind whipped around him, plunging him once more under Raric's dark spell.

Chapter Fifteen

"My dear, you know it's possible he's not alive anymore," Elistair said gently as Ethan paced the floor in the great hall. For days, the soldiers had scoured the woods and towns, searching for any sign of Owen or anyone who knew anything about the missing prince's whereabouts. But it was as if he had vanished into thin air. No one had seen him or anything suspicious, and no survivors had been recovered in the woods after the discovery on the forest path.

"He is," Ethan replied, sharper than he meant to. Owen was alive. He could feel it. "I will find him, Nomy. I have to."

Sonia suddenly came hurrying in, breaking into a hopeful smile. "We found her!"

"Found who?" Ethan asked with a frown.

"I knew there was an old magic user in the town," Sonia said, coming to a stop in front of Elistair and Ethan. "When you told us that magic was involved, Nomy had the guards search for her. She's arrived!"

Ethan let out a sharp breath, turning to Elistair. "You didn't say anything."

"I didn't want to disappoint you if we were not able to find her," Elistair said kindly. "I'm sorry, my dear. But hopefully now we will get some answers about what may have happened. And, if he's alive, maybe we'll be able to find Owen."

Ethan gave Elistair a tight hug, then rushed past Sonia, out into the courtyard where the ruined carriage had been brought back. Standing next to the wreckage was an old woman, her tawny skin so wrinkled that it could have passed for tree bark. Her silver hair was tied up on her head, her body stooped over with age. But when she looked up at Ethan, her dark eyes were bright and quick. "Your Highness," she said, her voice creaky. She bowed, though it was hardly noticeable with her hunched body.

"Good afternoon," Ethan greeted. "My sister said you are a magic user."

"Oh yes. I was born with it, many years ago now," the woman said as Elistair and Sonia came out the door behind Ethan. "I have been a healer, traveling throughout Comorra most of my life."

"What is your name?" Ethan asked.

"Tsume, Your Highness."

Ethan nodded, then dropped to one knee so he could look up into the withered old woman's face. "Have you heard of the attack on the Thornwood royal family, Lady Tsume?"

"I have," the woman said, her dark eyes sad as she gazed at Ethan. "But the young prince was not found?"

"No," Ethan said. "The prince, Owen, is my... I want him to be... my fiancé."

"Ah," Tsume said with a knowing nod. "And you believe that he is alive."

"I know he is," Ethan said. "I can feel it."

Tsume smiled at that. "True love, is it?" Ethan nodded. "Ah, youth," she mused.

"Please," Ethan said, reaching out his hand beseechingly to her. "I will do anything to get him back. I will pay you anything you ask for."

"I do not know what I can do, Your Highness, but I will help in any way I can. I don't need your money," Tsume said, waving his hand away with her own. "To reunite you with your heart would be payment enough."

Ethan smiled gratefully. "You are too kind, Lady Tsume."

Tsume gave him a chuckle. "I was once young and in love too, my prince. Now, what questions did you have for me?"

"The guards and the king and queen were killed by what appeared to be animals," Ethan said, rising to his feet again and gesturing Tsume over to the remains of the carriage. "We found three large wolves at the edge of the cliff by the river, with blood on their muzzles. But we also found this." He gestured to the scorch mark on the side of the carriage wood. "Do you know what might have caused this mark?"

Tsume studied the blackened wood closely, then ran her gnarled fingers over it. "Dark magic," she whispered. "Something evil."

"Are there any dark magic users in Comorra?"

Tsume looked thoughtful for a moment before she replied, "Not in Comorra. But in The Wilds, there is. The Banished One. The Shapeshifter Wizard. Magician of Darkness."

From behind them, Elistair let out a sharp breath. "Raric."

Tsume nodded gravely. Ethan turned to Elistair in surprise. "Who is Raric?"

"He was once King Stephan's advisor," Elistair said. "But he grew greedy and corrupt, studying dark magic. He planned to kill Stephan and wed Amelia to take Thornwood shortly after Owen was born. Stephan had him banished. The last I had heard of him, he was in Ubertlund. But that was years ago. I think Stephan assumed he was dead."

"You think this Raric is who did this to King Stephan and Queen Amelia, and took Owen?" Ethan asked. Elistair nodded grimly.

Tsume tapped her lips thoughtfully. "He has not been here long. I suspect he was planning the attack for when the king and queen left at the end of the summer."

"Where has he been staying?" Ethan asked, his hand automatically flying to the hilt of the sword strapped to his hip.

"Ethan!" Elistair protested. "You can't just rush out there on your own."

"I will," Ethan said firmly. "If Owen is out there, I have to save him."

"He has powerful magic," Tsume warned, her gravelly voice going even lower. "He can transform himself into any manner of human or beast. Do not underestimate him, young prince."

"I won't," Ethan said. "Tell me what you know. Please," he added hastily, bowing his head gratefully at Tsume again.

Tsume nodded. "I felt his presence this summer when the king and queen arrived at the castle for the summer visit. I can sense his magic, feel his dark power. It is like smoke on the wind." She stared thoughtfully at the sky. "It came from the north, where The Wilds begin. Somewhere in that forest, before the sea."

Ethan's heart picked up in his chest. That gave him a place to search, and he might still find Owen alive. He turned to Elistair and Sonia. "I must go search for him."

"You shouldn't go on your own," Elistair said sternly.

"Soldiers will only slow me down. I can search faster by myself," Ethan said pointedly.

"Ethan, I know you can defend yourself, but you are taking an enormous risk," Sonia said, her hands on her hips.

"I would risk everything to find Owen," Ethan said firmly. "If he's out there, I will find him and bring him back."

Elistair looked like they were going to protest further, but they finally just nodded. "I know your heart, my dear. And I know if he is out there, you will find him. Let us have supplies prepared, and you can leave in the morning at first light."

That would have to be good enough. Ethan turned to Tsume, dropping to his knee once more and taking her hand, holding it tightly with both of his own. "Thank you, Lady Tsume," he said. "You have my eternal gratitude, and that of Comorra."

Tsume smiled softly and squeezed his hands. "Find your true love, my prince, and bring him home."

The servants prepared two horses for Ethan, one for him to ride, and one with supplies. The woods were expansive, but, as Ethan had said, searching on his own would be much faster than trying to command a group of soldiers. He hoped he could cover the entire northern forest area in only a few days at most. He prepared his bow and a quiver full of arrows, and he sharpened his sword. Tsume's words about Raric's ability to transform into any type of beast echoed in his mind. Would he know Raric in a non-human form if he saw him? Or could the sorcerer approach him as something so innocuous that he would not know until it was too late? Would Raric even see him as a threat? What was he doing to Owen? That last thought made it hard for Ethan to breathe. If Raric wanted the throne of Thornwood, what might he do to Owen in order to get it?

Ethan forced himself to get a few hours of sleep before he ate a quick meal and then swung up onto his horse. He bid farewell to Elistair and Sonia, promising to return as soon as he found Owen, and he would send word back to the castle if he encountered any towns in the forest that could deliver news. And then he and his two horses took off toward the forest path, just as the sun crested the sky and flooded the world with light.

Chapter Sixteen

The weather was growing colder. Owen wondered what would happen if winter came and he was still under Raric's curse. Surely the sorcerer wouldn't let him freeze to death. Maybe he expected that Owen would choose self-preservation before then. Owen knew that was going to be a hard choice. But he was not going to let Raric break his resolve. If he wanted Thornwood, he was going to have to take it from Owen by force.

Alli and Sir William tried to be positive after Raric found the letter, but Owen could see that they were just as discouraged as he was. Alli had snuck back into the ruins to poke around, but there was nothing helpful that she could find. "Do you think, if you flew back to the castle as a swan, that Ethan would recognize you somehow?" Alli asked hopefully.

"I don't know," Owen said. He wanted to think that Ethan would recognize him in any form, but this type of magic was so rare, it might not even occur to Ethan that Owen might not be in a human form. And even if he did realize that it was Owen under the swan guise, what then? Owen couldn't speak to tell Ethan how to break the curse; he would have to return to the lake in order to turn into a human again. The only thing he could think of was trying to steal the page from Raric's spell book and bring it to the castle, but Raric had sealed off the tower further with some sort of enchantment that didn't even allow Owen to fly close enough to look in the window anymore. He was running out of options.

"If we can get to a town, perhaps we could find someone to kiss me and break my curse," Sir William said thoughtfully. "Then I can relay your plight."

Alli let out a huff of laughter. "No one is going to just kiss a salamander, Willie. And even if they do, it's supposed to be a virgin. That's kind of specific."

"I can be very persuasive," Sir William said, opening his dark eyes wide in what they assumed was an attempt to be endearing but really just made him look confused.

"They're more likely to kiss me," Alli said, smacking her tail to send water flying. "At least I'm cute and fluffy."

"Well, fluffy," Sir William muttered.

Alli ignored him. "What do you think, Owen?"

Owen sighed, trying to not feel defeated. "That might be our best option. Perhaps if we can find another magic user, they will recognize the magic for what it is."

"Worth a try," Alli said, bouncing a bit. "We run away and search for a town until we find one with a magic user?"

"You don't have to come with," Owen said. "There are hunters and trappers out there. I don't want to put you or Sir William in danger."

Sir William huffed. "I would sacrifice my life to protect you, Your Highness!"

"You're our friend," Alli agreed. "We're not going to make you face this on your own!"

Owen smiled gratefully. "You both are wonderful."

Alli slid out of the water and shook out her fur, sending water droplets scattering in the sunlight. "Come on! Let's go before that wizard sees us!"

Sir William climbed onto Alli's back, and Owen flapped his wings to get off the ground. He didn't want to fly too high with hunters about; keeping low seemed like a wiser choice, even if it was slower. Together, the three plunged into the forest.

Ethan's first day of searching had turned up nothing. He had only made camp for the night when it became too dark to see anything in the woods, and he had barely slept, keeping one eye out for any sort of approaching creature that could possibly be the dark sorcerer. As soon as dawn came, he quickly ate and then continued on his search. He didn't know what he was looking for. He hoped he would know it when he saw it. He debated calling out to Owen, but he didn't know if that might draw Raric into his path either. So, he continued his search in silence, looking for anything that might give him an idea of where to go next.

It was after noon when he stopped again just long enough to eat. He did not want to waste much time, but he also knew he wouldn't be able to face a potential foe if he did not take care of himself. He had seen a few animals running through the woods, but for the most part, they seemed to be avoiding him. He suspected that they were used to staying away from humans, as most of them in this area would be hunters. He wondered if Owen was being properly cared for. When he found him, he would take Owen back to the castle and make sure that the cook made every single one of Owen's favorite dishes for him. He wanted to make sure that Owen never had an unfulfilled desire again in his life. He had already messed that up before, and while Owen's words had stung, they had been true. He had not thought about Owen's feelings. He had been selfish. He was a prince. He had to think beyond himself, to the good of his partner, his people, and his kingdom.

Owen followed Alli through the trees. Alli had a better sense of smell than he did and would probably have a better idea where the nearest town was. He flew around a tree trunk, then frowned to himself. He could see something a distance away. Something bright blue that looked out of place in the forest. He pulled up short, quickly fluttering into the branches of a tree in case it was a hunter. But after a few moments, the figure didn't move, and Owen was able to make out that the person had their back to him. That was a relief, at least. He silently swooped down, hiding amongst the foliage as he drew closer.

The royal blue was one of the colors of the Comorran royal family. Perhaps a guard or a knight or a noble. He moved closer still, only a short distance away now, before the figure shifted to put something into the pack resting at his feet, and Owen caught a look at the profile. It was Ethan! He nearly bolted out of the trees toward him, until he spotted Ethan's bow and the quiver of arrows within easy reach. He couldn't approach him this way without risking Ethan possibly shooting him. He remembered the accuracy of Ethan taking down the fox when they went hunting, and his stomach churned.

But Ethan was here, in the forest, so close to him. He had to be searching for him. There was no other reason for the Comorran prince to be this far north, and especially not alone. There were no signs of soldiers or another encampment. At least he did not have to worry about a company of soldiers also taking shots at him, but he still had to be cautious.

The hair on the back of Ethan's neck stood up. Something was watching him; he could feel it. Whatever it was was not moving. He stood up from the log where he sat, pulling his sword out from its scabbard as casually as he could, turning it as if he were examining the edge. It was not as reflective as a mirror, but he could see the glint of golden sunlight off of something in the trees. He turned slowly, as if scanning his surroundings. The branch he had seen something on was empty, but the leaves rustled, as if something had only just been there. He sheathed his sword, heart racing, as he scooped up his bow from the ground, readying an arrow. If something was stalking him right now, he didn't want to be distracted by getting on his horse. Better to continue on foot for a bit until he knew what he was facing.

Owen peered cautiously around the tree branch. Ethan had picked up his bow and arrow and was moving silently through the woods. Owen swallowed hard. It was still several hours until sunset. He had to keep Ethan nearby so he could find him once he transformed. But

Ethan was aware of something near him, and every moment that Owen stayed nearby risked him being shot. He waited until Ethan had walked past him and was barely visible amongst the trees before he soared off the branch and into the brush to where Alli and Sir William were crouched, watching. "That's Ethan!" he said, keeping his voice low.

Alli blinked in surprise. "It is? He's cute!"

Owen nodded. "He must be looking for me."

"How romantic!" Alli said with a dreamy sigh.

"It will not be romantic if he shoots Owen out of the sky," Sir William pointed out.

"We need to draw him close to the lake," Owen said, watching the trees where Ethan had disappeared. "But not so soon that he tries to investigate the ruins." He could only imagine what Raric might do if he came back to find Prince Ethan of Comorra snooping around the building. "But he's a really good hunter. We have to be very careful." He cautiously spread his wings and followed after where Ethan had gone.

The sun glinted off of something moving in the trees, and Ethan shaded his eyes to look. Something wove in and out of the branches nearby, slow and cautious, like it was trying not to be seen. His heart thumped in his chest. Could that be Raric, stalking him? What form would the sorcerer take to try to deceive him or overwhelm him? Would Raric even know who he was or what he was there for? Ethan glanced around, trying not to let his eyes linger too long in the direction the reflection had come from. Something was definitely following him. Something with large wings. He walked for a few more moments before he suddenly whirled around again, scanning the trees.

Settling onto a branch a short distance away was an elegant, white swan. Ethan's eyes narrowed. Swans were not entirely unusual around this area, but they should be preparing to fly to warmer climates for the winter. This one was very obviously following him, from the way that it froze when its eyes met his own. Ethan lifted the bow, leveling the arrow toward the swan.

Something slammed into his ankle, knocking him off balance, and the arrow went wide, soaring off into the trees. Ethan looked down in time to see a furry otter tail disappear into the brush. When he looked up again, the swan had vanished. He muttered softly to himself, pulling another arrow from its quiver, scanning the trees for any sign of movement.

Owen darted through the branches as fast as he could. A few moments later, he heard Alli in the underbrush and slowed to a stop, his heart pounding. He glanced back, but it did not seem like Ethan was following them. "Thank you," he breathed to Alli.

Alli nodded, glancing around. "I know we're trying not to lose him, but I think it might be harder than we think."

"We are not far from the lake," Sir William said, pointing one of his tiny toes into the distance. "If we can keep him in this area for a little while, we should be able to lure him there when the moon comes up."

A snap of branches nearby sent the three of them scattering. Owen darted into a thicket, barely concealing himself before Ethan appeared, his bow held ready, his shoulders tensed for an attack he sensed would come. Owen wished he could do something to reassure Ethan that he was here, that he was safe. But if Ethan knew anything about Raric or that magic was involved in his disappearance, of course he would be cautious about anything that might be following him. On their hunt, he had not even seen the beautiful fox before Ethan had shot it. That thought kept him frozen in place, barely breathing, for several minutes after Ethan had disappeared into the forest once more.

Alli and Sir William appeared by his side. "All right, Owen?" Alli whispered.

"Yes," Owen breathed, looking down at the otter sadly. "He'll kill me if he finds me. He probably thinks I'm Raric or one of his spies."

"Have no fear, Your Highness!" Sir William declared. "We shall keep him busy until you can reveal yourself to him!"

"Please be careful," Owen pleaded. If Alli or Sir William got hurt, he would never forgive himself.

"You stay here," Alli instructed. "I'll keep up with him and bring him back here when the sun starts to set."

"Thank you," Owen said gratefully. Alli gave his cheek a soft nuzzle before she darted into the bushes again, Sir William following after her, leaving Owen alone once more. Tears stung his eyes. He couldn't blame Ethan for not recognizing him, but it still hurt that his first time seeing Ethan since his rather tumultuous departure was with Ethan trying to kill him, even unknowingly. He had already lost so much. He did not want to cause the young man any more grief. He just wanted Ethan to hold him, to reassure him that everything would be all right, that they would figure things out together. But instead, he sat hidden in the thicket, nervously waiting for his best friends to return.

Chapter Seventeen

It felt like forever but was probably only an hour or two before Alli and Sir William came charging back through the underbrush. "Ready?" Alli asked. Owen sucked in a breath and nodded. "Wait for my signal," Alli said just as Ethan appeared in their line of sight again. Alli grabbed a few of the bright red berries on the bush over Owen's head and squished them, smearing the sticky mess on her chest. She nodded to Owen before she stumbled out of the bush, staggering dramatically, wheezing and gasping as her tiny paw clutched her chest. Ethan saw her and moved cautiously closer, holding his bow and arrow loosely in his grip. Alli flopped onto the ground and lay still, not even a whisker moving. Ethan stepped closer still, then gave the little otter a nudge with the toe of his boot.

Alli sprang up, darting between his feet. Ethan yelped and spun, his arrow skittering across the ground as he tripped over his own boots and landed in a heap. "Go!" Alli shouted, and Owen burst from the bush, flapping as hard as his wings would carry him toward the ruins, Sir William frantically clinging to his back.

Owen burst out of the trees. He had never been so happy to see the lake in his life. He quickly swooped up to rest on one of the large stones further down the shoreline, crouching down so Ethan would not easily see him. Sir William slid off of him just as Alli broke through the trees and scrambled up the rocks after them. "Are you all right?" she asked.

"Never better," Sir William said grumpily.

"I'm fine," Owen replied. "You?"

"I'm good. That boy of yours can move!" Alli declared.

"I know," Owen said, glancing up at the sky. The last of the sunlight had faded, and the moon was just making itself visible over the tree line.

Ethan stepped from the trees onto the shore of what appeared to be a large lake. At the center of it was an island, with a large building on it. It looked to be abandoned, no lights shining from it, but he still kept his bow and arrow ready, heart pounding in his chest. Where had the swan disappeared to?

The moonlight was about to touch the water. Owen took a deep breath. It was now or never. He lifted himself off the rock, his large wings spread, to land gracefully on the surface of the lake. Across the water, he could see Ethan staring in surprise at the animal coming forward so willingly when he stood there, bow poised. He wanted to say something, anything, but he worried if he made any sort of sudden sound, Ethan might consider that a threat and shoot. So instead, he simply rested on the water, the gentle waves creating a rocking motion, as he gazed mournfully back at Ethan with his round eyes. He waited for the familiar swish of water and the dizziness, but it did not come.

Where was the moon? He had seen it only moments ago. He turned his head up and felt panic surge through him. A bank of clouds had covered the moon, blocking the light from falling on the lake. He turned back toward Ethan desperately, his heart sinking when he saw that Ethan had drawn back the bowstring.

Something splashed loudly into the water nearby. It was Alli, jumping and slapping at the water, trying frantically to get Ethan's attention off of Owen. She chittered and screeched, popping in and out of the water in a desperate bid for attention. The splashing only distracted Ethan for a moment before his arrow swiveled back, aimed straight at Owen's heart.

Owen squeezed his eyes shut, not wanting to see Ethan's arrow come for him. But suddenly he felt a rush of water around him, lifting him from his webbed feet. The familiar dizziness struck him, and then he felt the solid ground under his boots, water lapping at his legs. He peeked his eyes open, half expecting to see an arrow protruding from his chest. But Ethan still stood on the bank, bow and arrow raised and taut, pointed at him, staring in shock. Owen stayed still, hardly daring to breathe.

Ethan's hands shook, and he lowered the weapon as the water slipped away into ripples around Owen's feet. At first, he wondered if his eyes were playing tricks on him, that he was so desperate for any sign of his almost-fiancé that he was simply imagining him. But then Owen slowly held out a hand to him. "Hello, Ethan."

The bow and arrow fell from Ethan's hand, hitting the muddy ground. Ethan dashed into the water, wrapping his arms around Owen's waist to lift him up and spin him around, pressing his lips to Owen's in a desperate kiss. Owen kissed him back, feeling tears start to flow down his face as he gripped Ethan's shoulders with both hands.

Ethan finally broke the kiss to stare down into Owen's eyes. "I knew you were alive," he breathed, his voice barely above a whisper. "No one else believed me."

Owen smiled, reaching up to stroke his cheek gently. "I could never leave you."

Ethan turned his head to kiss Owen's palm lovingly before he scooped him up into his arms, water flowing off of Owen's boots, and he carried the blond prince back to the shore in his arms. Owen nestled into them, perfectly content to let Ethan hold him close for now.

Once they were back on land, Ethan carried Owen over to a log and set him down, then knelt in front of him, pushing his blond hair out of his face, as if checking for injuries. "Are you hurt? What happened to you?" His dark eyes were brimming with tears, and Owen reached up to wipe them away with his thumb.

"I'm all right," he said softly. "But Raric attacked us and killed my mother and the soldiers."

Ethan nodded solemnly. "We found them. But we didn't find you. Everyone said you were dead in the woods somewhere, but I didn't believe it."

"Were there any other survivors?" Owen asked hopefully.

Ethan shook his head, giving Owen's hands a gentle squeeze. "No," he said, his voice tender. "I'm so sorry." Owen nodded, bowing his head. He had expected as much, but now he knew for sure. "Did Raric do this?" Ethan asked, gesturing to the lake behind them.

Owen nodded again. "He has me under a spell."

Ethan instantly looked concerned. "What kind of a spell?"

Owen glanced up at the sliver of moonlight overhead. "I'm only able to be human as long as the moonlight is touching the lake. When the sun comes up, I turn into a swan until the moon returns."

Ethan frowned darkly. "Why?"

Owen sighed and squeezed Ethan's hand. "Raric is trying to force me to marry him. Then he can legally rule Thornwood by my side. And if anything were to happen to me, he would be the one who would take over."

Ethan gritted his teeth. "So, he'd probably get rid of you once you married him." Owen inhaled as he nodded. "I won't let that happen," Ethan declared, rising sharply to his feet. "I will kill him for what he did to you and your family."

"No," Owen said, following him up and grabbing Ethan's arms to hold him. "If he dies before the spell is lifted, I won't be able to change back into a human."

"What do we have to do to break the curse?" Ethan asked.

"I found his book of spells. You must make a vow of eternal love."

"I make it!" Ethan said, dropping to one knee again and taking both of Owen's hands in his own. "You are my true love, now and forever."

Owen shook his head sadly. "You have to prove it, not only in word, but in deed."

Ethan stared at him blankly, and Owen was sure he did not look any less confused. "How do I do that?" Ethan asked.

"I don't know," Owen said, clutching his hands tightly.

"Can I take you back to the palace with me?" Ethan asked. "Even if you are a swan?"

Owen swallowed hard. "I don't know what Raric would do if you took me away. I don't want you to be hurt, or to put anyone else in danger."

"Let him come," Ethan snarled, rising to his feet and reaching for his sword.

"No!" Owen protested, grabbing his arm. "Please. He's too powerful. He might kill you." He had already lost so much. If Raric struck down Ethan too, Owen was sure he would break into a million pieces.

Ethan was silent for a long moment, thinking. "I will leave a horse for you. A half mile east from here. When you turn human tomorrow, take the horse and ride as fast as you can to the palace. You should arrive just before dawn. I will be waiting for you, and when you arrive, I will marry you. I will make a vow of eternal love in front of the whole kingdom."

Owen gasped softly, reaching up to touch Ethan's cheek. "You would do that for me?"

"I would do anything for you," Ethan replied firmly, holding him close. "I love you."

Owen sniffed, standing up on his tiptoes to kiss Ethan eagerly. "I missed you."

Ethan stroked his hair gently. "I missed you. And I want to apologize."

"For what?" Owen asked.

"For what an ass I was," Ethan said, taking one of Owen's hands in both of his own to clutch it tightly. "You were right. I was selfish and didn't think enough about you and your needs. And for that, I'm sorry."

Owen's heart gave a leap in his chest. Their whole spat before he had left Comorra's palace didn't seem as important now, but it still felt good to hear Ethan say the words. "I forgive you," he said. "I want to spend my life with you, Ethan."

Ethan beamed, holding him close. "I want you, so badly. I want to spend my life showing you how much I love you and how sorry I am."

Ethan leaned down and pressed his lips firmly to Owen's, holding him close. Owen's fingers tangled into Ethan's jacket, clutching him like he would never let go. "I promise that after tomorrow night, we will never be apart again," Ethan whispered in his ear.

Owen kissed him eagerly again before pulling back. "Go," he said. "If he catches you here, I don't know what he will do."

Ethan reluctantly stepped back. "Will you be all right until tomorrow?"

"Yes," Owen assured him. "He wants my kingdom, he won't hurt me."

Ethan nodded, pulling him in for another long kiss before reluctantly drawing back. "Tomorrow," he promised.

"Tomorrow," Owen agreed.

"I love you." Ethan gave his cheek a last stroke with his fingertips before he snatched up his discarded bow and arrow, turned, and vanished into the woods.

Owen felt like his heart might break, watching Ethan leave him again. But he would rather die than let harm come to Ethan too. He had held out this long against Raric, he could hold out another night. And then Ethan would marry him in front of all of Comorra and free him from Raric's spell. That thought made his aching spirit lift as he waited at the edge of the lake for the dawn.

Chapter Eighteen

It was hours after Ethan's departure when Raric appeared. Owen's heart beat faster at the man's approach, but he forced his face into a cold mask of indifference. "Hello, little princeling," Raric said as Owen rose to his feet from the log he was sitting on.

Owen just glared at him. Raric chuckled. "Oh, Owen. If only you knew how much your rejection hurts me."

Owen did not believe that for a second. "What do you want?"

"Have you changed your mind?" Raric asked.

"Every night you ask me, and every night I give you the same answer. I'll die first."

Raric smirked before the look became even more smug. "I suppose it's easy to act brave when you plan to escape again."

"What are you talking about?" Owen asked, feeling his mouth go dry.

"'Come to the castle tomorrow night. I will marry you and make a vow of eternal love in front of the whole kingdom,'" Raric said with a cold smile. "So sweet of your dear Comorran prince."

Owen gasped and lunged for him, but Raric threw up a hand, and Owen stumbled backward, hitting the ground hard as pain lanced over his skin. Raric laughed. "Such spirit, princeling. It's a shame you will not be able to attend the wedding."

Owen glowered as he struggled to his feet, tasting blood on the inside of his mouth. "I will marry Ethan and break this spell. You'll have to kill me if you want to stop me."

"Oh no, I don't have to do any such thing," Raric said, and something evil glinted like fire in his eyes. "You see, you've forgotten one very important thing." He raised his hand, extending one long, pale finger to point upward. "Tomorrow night, there is no moon."

Owen whirled around to stare at the sliver of moon high above them amongst the blinking stars. The moon was barely visible. Raric was right. Tomorrow was the new moon.

Raric wrapped his hand around the silver locket. Black lightning crackled, momentarily blinding Owen. When he could see again, he found himself gazing back into his own face. Bright blue eyes, pale blond hair, smooth features, even down to the freckle on his right temple. The only difference that he could see was that, where his own clothing was white, this other figure wore black. The other Owen stared back at him, mirroring his shocked expression, before a grin that he recognized all too well from Raric spread over the other man's face. "What do you think, little prince?" he asked, spinning in a circle. His own voice coming out of Raric's mouth made Owen shudder. "Do you think your fiancé will like it?"

"You stay away from him!" Owen lunged at Raric, but the sorcerer easily avoided the movement.

"I should have thought of this sooner," Raric said, brushing his hand through the blond hair that rested at his temples. "But this is even better than I planned. By marrying the prince of Comorra, disguised as the crown prince of Thornwood, I'll be able to rule both kingdoms."

Owen stifled a cry at that. His second family, the only people he had left in the world now, were in grave danger, and he could do nothing to help them. He turned back to Raric, fire in his blue eyes. "If you harm any of them, I swear I will kill you."

"Oh no, Your Highness, you won't get that chance. You see..." Raric gave another spin on his heel, showing off his form as Owen. "When your dear prince pledges his eternal love to another," he dropped his voice into a low, conspiratorial whisper, "you will die."

Owen gasped as Raric let out a cackle that made all of the hair on his body stand up in horror. "No!"

Raric shrugged and gave Owen a grin. "Sorry, little prince. You made your choice when you refused me. Don't worry, I'll take good care of Prince Ethan."

Owen let out an anguished cry that was cut short as Raric waved a hand. The world spun, and Owen was plunged into blackness.

He hadn't wanted to leave Owen alone; every fiber of his being screamed at him to hold the blond close and never let him go. But Tsume and Elistair's warnings had echoed in Ethan's head. Facing Raric alone sounded like a fool's errand. At least at the castle, he had Captain Xan and the guards to back him up. And Owen had been right. Who knew what Raric might do if he caught Ethan hovering around his captured prize? Obviously, the dark sorcerer had no qualms about killing royalty.

Sonia had asked Tsume to stay in the palace until Ethan returned, taking Owen's suggestion to write down the knowledge she possessed that could perhaps be used one day when science had to be relied on for healing instead of magic. Tsume had agreed, with the caveat that she would still see patients in need of her healing while she was there. Ethan found both of them in the library when he returned, despite the early-morning hour. He hurried in, dropping into the chair next to them. "What do you know of turning people into animals?"

"Ethan!" Sonia scolded, and Ethan flushed slightly.

"My apologies, Lady Tsume," he said, bowing his head at the woman. "I found Owen. But there is a curse on him. He turns into a swan by day and is only human by night."

"Oh!" Sonia gasped, her hand flying to her mouth. "Poor Owen!"

"Transfiguring others against their will is difficult," Tsume said, the barest hint of a shudder wracking her hunched form. "Raric is indeed a powerful magician."

"Would you be able to lift the curse if I brought Owen here?" Ethan asked, already prepping to run out the door and ride all the way back to Owen's side.

Tsume looked grave as she considered this. "Dark magic is not something to be trifled with," she said solemnly. "Trying to remove the curse if one is not the caster could have dire repercussions for all involved." At least that made Ethan feel less guilty for leaving Owen behind again, though it did nothing to assuage his nervousness.

"He said that the curse can be broken if his true love proves his eternal love in word and deed. I left him a horse to ride to the palace after he turns human tonight, before the sun rises tomorrow morning. I told him I would marry him. Would that break the curse?"

Sonia looked like she wanted to squeal in delight but was holding it back, just clearing her throat and turning to Tsume for the answer.

Tsume tapped her slender finger against her lips. "I would think so, though magic is not exact. It follows its own rules, especially dark magic. That is part of the reason it is so dangerous. But if your intentions are pure, I would think that marrying him would break such a spell."

Ethan let out a breath, taking her hand and squeezing it lightly. "Thank you, Lady Tsume."

"Did you find Raric too?" Sonia asked worriedly.

Ethan shook his head. "No. I wanted to stay with Owen, but he told me to go, that Raric was dangerous."

"Why does he have Owen anyway?" Sonia asked, twirling her quill uneasily, spreading black ink over her fingertips.

Ethan grimaced. "He wants Owen to marry him so he can legally be the ruler of Thornwood, marrying the heir."

"Which means he would be second in line to the throne," Sonia said, heaving a heavy sigh.

Ethan suppressed a shudder. "Yes."

Elistair suddenly came rushing into the library, nearly tripping over their robes, elaborate hairstyle tumbling loose from its many pins and braids. "Ethan!" they gasped, leaning down to embrace the prince tightly. "Thank the heavens you are safe!"

"Yes, Nomy," Ethan said, giving them a hug in return. "I'm all right, and I found Owen!" He quickly relayed the story again of finding Owen, the curse upon him, and his plan for the impromptu marriage ceremony. Elistair immediately agreed that they and Sonia would handle the hasty preparations, sending Ethan to get a few hours of rest.

The grand ballroom was decorated with flowers and hanging silks, and the servants all began to help the cooks prepare a magnificent feast. Messengers were sent throughout the land, inviting commoners and nobles alike to the palace at sundown for an all-night party in honor of Prince Ethan finding his lost love.

As the crowd gathered, Ethan wasn't able to keep himself from pacing. He loved Owen and wanted to be with him forever. If something went wrong, he knew his heart would not recover. Not now that he had finally found Owen again and could do something to help him. He had nearly lost Owen twice before. He was not going to make that mistake again.

Chapter Nineteen

The room he was in was dark when Owen finally awoke. There were no windows and only the faintest bit of light under the bottom of the door. When his vision finally adjusted, he was able to make out several old pieces of furniture and trinkets scattered about. He seemed to be in an old storeroom. He was also in his swan form again. Tears pricked his eyes as he made his way around the room, trying to find anything that might help, anything that could be a way out, but there was nothing.

"Owen!" he heard Alli call from beyond the door. "Are you in there?"

"Yes." His voice sounded shaky and hoarse from tears, even to himself. "But the door is locked, and there's nothing in here to open it with."

"Hold on," Alli called. "We'll get you out!"

Sir William flattened down and tried to squirm under the gap the way he had to get into the tower, but this door came much closer to the floor, and there was no way he would be able to slide under it. He gave the door a ferocious kick with his tiny hind foot, but the door remained as solid as ever. "We'll get you out, Your Highness, never fear!" he declared. "Sir William Farthington is at your service!"

Alli studied the wooden door critically before her dark, beady eyes landed on the hinges that held the door to the wall. The metal peg that held the pieces together was already poking out from the bottom hinge. She grasped it with her tiny otter fingers and pulled. It started to slide. She tugged again, and the peg came free, the bottom hinge settling onto itself. She gave an excited hop. "Look!" she squealed.

"Ah hah!" Sir William declared. "Good work, my fine otter friend! Can you reach the second one?"

Alli stood on her hind legs and stretched up her tiny arms, barely able to flick the middle hinge. "No."

Sir William glanced around, then spotted a large, ornate chair covered in dust about ten feet away. He scurried toward it, then planted his back against one of the carved legs and pushed. The chair barely budged. Alli scampered next to him and wrapped her tail around one of the other legs, giving a heave. The chair scooted a few inches. "Yes! Onward!" Sir William declared, shoving at the chair, and Alli began to pull again. It was slow progress, but eventually the chair reached the wooden door. Alli scrambled up onto the seat, able to reach the center hinge peg now. It took a little working with her claws, but she pulled the second one free. "Owen, can you push the door open on your right?" she called.

The door gave a little shiver as he attempted it, but it did not move. "No," Owen replied.

"Don't worry, we'll get the last one," Alli said, scrambling onto the carved back of the chair and stretching up. She was barely able to reach the top of the peg, but this one was solid, holding the metal hinge plates securely. She pried at it with her tiny fingers, but it remained stubbornly in place. "It's stuck," she called.

"It probably needs some oil," Owen replied, despair starting to settle in his heart again. There might be oil somewhere in the building, but finding it would take time, and if it was behind another locked door, it would take even more time that they did not have.

Alli looked around in dismay. "Where would I find that?"

"I don't know," Owen said. "Maybe the stable, or in the tower?"

"Hurry up!" Sir William huffed from the floor.

"It's stuck," Alli replied, giving him a glare and fluffing out her thick fur. "We need some oil."

Sir William blinked his round, newty eyes before breaking into a delighted smile. "Stand aside, peasant, Sir William Farthington is on the job!" He suddenly clambered up the leg of the chair, onto the seat, then up the back. "Give me a boost."

Alli leaned down so Sir William could climb onto her head, stretching up so he was level with the door hinge. He eyed it critically for a moment before giving a delighted nod. "Haha, you shall not win today, fiend!" He turned his back to the connection and began to scratch his rough skin up and down over the stiff hinge.

"What are you doing?" Alli asked.

"I am secreting mucus," Sir William replied proudly, as if declaring he had slayed a dragon. "I always thought it might come in handy for something."

Alli wrinkled her nose. "That's gross," she said, but she held her head high for Sir William to dance and shimmy up and down the door hinge, the mucus from his lizard-like body working its way into the gaps between the metal. He made little sing-song noises as he did, dancing to a rhythm only he could hear, for several minutes before pulling away.

"Now, try again, and give that door what-for!"

Alli set Sir William down onto the arm of the chair before reaching up to wiggle and pull at the stubborn hinge. It gave a little, and she grasped it with her claws, tugging at it. It took several more minutes of jiggling and yanking, but finally the peg released from its position with a sudden pop, and the door sagged onto its unsupported hinges. Sir William let out a whoop and jumped down from the chair, trying to push it out of the way. Alli helped him, then turned back again. "Try again, Owen!"

The door teetered, and the next moment, swung outward on its lock. Owen squeezed out of the opening, his eyes shining with unshed tears. "You did it!" he declared, throwing his wings around Alli and Sir William.

Alli gave him a quick hug before pulling back. "Come on, we have to get you to your prince!"

Owen beamed. "Thank you, Alli. And Sir William, I promise after this I will give you a kiss."

Sir William perked up in delight. "You will? Oh, thank you, Owen! I would be forever in your debt."

Owen wasn't sure that he would be able to break the spell on the little salamander, but that was the least of his concerns right now. "Let's go!" he declared, unfurling his wings and giving a flap to lift himself up and out the nearest broken window. Alli snatched up Sir William in her mouth and scurried down the stairs after him.

Ethan continued to pace the ballroom nervously. What if Owen did not come? What if something had happened to him? Once the sun set, Ethan found himself counting down the hours, minutes, and seconds it would take Owen to find the horse he had left and ride to the palace. He wanted to rush out and find him, but he knew he had to be patient. If Owen could not start traveling until sundown, it would take several hours of hard riding to get to the castle. At least the weather was getting colder, the sun setting earlier, so there would be a little extra time, but not much. He had to make sure that he married Owen by the time the dawn rose, or else he risked losing Owen yet again. While no one would begrudge him keeping Owen close as a swan to protect him, it was not as if Owen could marry him or rule over a kingdom that way, and he did not want to subject his tender-hearted fiancé to such a fate.

Sonia and Elistair waited with him. Captain Xan had his guards prepared should Raric come after Owen. Whether the magician would be foolhardy enough to try to attack Comorra was in question, but no one wanted to underestimate what the crafty, old wizard might do.

The early morning hours were approaching, and the assembled crowd ate and drank and danced as they waited for Prince Owen to arrive. Ethan glanced out the large windows. Was it only his imagination, or was the sky already getting lighter? His heart thundered in his chest. Sonia squeezed his hand next to him. "He'll come," she whispered in reassurance.

Ethan nodded, chewing on his lower lip as he stared at the sky, willing the darkness to stay as long as possible.

"Prince Owen of Thornwood," came the sudden announcement above the din from the chamberlain at the door, and the room fell silent, all eyes turning. Ethan whirled around, heart skipping a beat in his chest.

Owen stood in the doorway, in a radiant outfit of red and black silk. His blond hair was windswept from his ride, the burning candles and firelight playing over their white-blond strands. Ethan smiled, feeling relief wash over him. Owen had come. He was here, and he was safe.

Owen stepped inside the room, and the crowd bowed in waves as he slowly walked between them. His head was high, and Ethan was surprised to see that, despite his petite stature, he seemed to be looking down his nose at everyone in the room, as if all were below him. He had never seen such a haughty expression on Owen's face before. He swallowed nervously. Owen had lost his family and been trapped for a long time under Raric's curse with no one to help him, so perhaps he was not feeling as warm toward people as he used to be. Owen silently crossed the ballroom through the path the crowd made to Ethan on the dais.

Ethan held up his hand as Owen reached the stairs, and Owen climbed them, placing his own hand into it. Ethan beamed and pulled him close. "I worried you wouldn't come."

"Nothing could keep me away," Owen replied.

"Are you all right? Something about you seems different," Ethan said cautiously, as if afraid to give voice to the words.

Owen gave him a bright smile. "Don't worry. After tonight, everything will be fine."

Ethan smiled back, reaching up to brush his thumb over Owen's cheek. "I love you."

Owen leaned into the touch, reaching up to hold Ethan's bicep through his jacket. "I know."

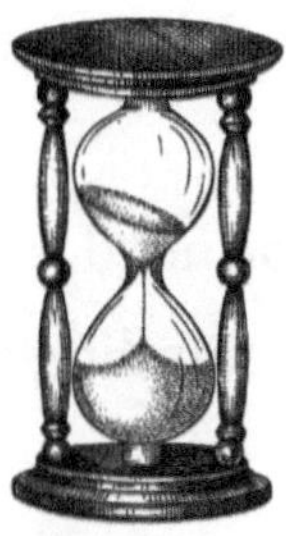

Owen spotted the horse with the royal insignia on its side being escorted by a groom to the nearby stables, and his heart stuttered in his chest. He dove into the trees, finding Alli and Sir William after a moment. "Raric's already here," he moaned breathlessly.

"We still have time," Alli said confidently. "If you can get inside, I'm sure Ethan will know it's you."

"Are the windows open?" Sir William asked. It was so cold outside, Owen suspected all of the windows had been securely locked.

"I'll go check," he said anyway and swooped upward toward the castle in the hopes of finding one open somewhere to let out the heat and smoke from the fireplaces. Several guards watched him curiously, as he was sure a swan flying around the palace was unusual, but he couldn't focus on them. He headed for the glowing windows of the grand ballroom, praying that at least one of them might be unlatched. The first few did not yield, and he swooped around to the other side before stopping short in midair. Raric, still in Owen's form, stood on the dais next to Ethan, holding onto his arm.

Ethan raised a hand, and the room fell silent. "Gentlefolk, good nobles. My dear Nomy." Ethan cast a beaming smile across the room where Elistair sat on an elaborate throne. "I have a most important announcement." He turned his gaze back to Owen. "I have found my lost love, and today, in front of the whole kingdom, I wish to marry him."

The crowd cheered and applauded. Elistair smiled and waved their hand at the minister who was standing off to the side in preparation. "So shall it be!"

Outside the palace, Owen swooped, beating his wings against the glass, but it was solid, and no one could hear the frantic slam of his wings over the roar of the crowd. Every single window was latched tight against the cold. He thought he might have been able to crack one if he tried hard enough, but the glass was thick, and he was more likely to slice himself to ribbons than to break into the ballroom.

He swooped lower to the ground, finding Alli and Sir William emerging from the moat. "There has to be a way in," Alli said worriedly.

"Have we tried the front door?" Sir William asked.

"Yes, the guards will just let a swan waddle right into the palace," Alli said with a roll of her eyes. "We need like a secret way in where no one will see us."

Owen's head shot up. "The gardens!" he gasped. The hidden escape that Ethan and he had used all that time ago to steal away into the night to be alone together. "This way!" He flapped toward the garden, Alli and Sir William hurrying after him. It took him a few moments to find the correct pedestal amongst all of the similar-looking ones, but he finally found the nearby bench and counted two down. He threw his weight against the large vase of flowers until it tipped to the side, opening the trap door with a squeak.

Sir William let out a whoop of delight. "Yes! Go, Owen! Stop this wedding!"

Chapter Twenty

"Do you, Prince Owen of Thornwood, take Prince Ethan of Comorra, to be your lawfully wedded husband for as long as you both shall live?" the minister droned.

"I do," Owen said, giving Ethan a sticky sweet smile.

The minister turned to Ethan with a nod. "You had your own vow to make, Your Highness?"

"Yes." Ethan took both of Owen's in his, squeezing them lightly. His eyes were soft and glimmered with the barest hint of tears. "Owen. When I lost you, my heart broke. I thought I would never get the chance to tell you how I really felt. But now, before the whole kingdom, I make a vow to you. A vow of eternal love. I love you now, and I will love you forever." He stepped in, sliding his hand up to catch the back of Owen's blond hair with his fingers, pressing their lips together.

Owen did not return the kiss. When Ethan pulled back, Owen was smirking, a look so unfamiliar on his pretty face that it took Ethan a moment to understand it. He opened his mouth to ask if everything was all right when there was a sudden crash behind him. A few screams came from the crowd, as a large, white swan suddenly fell mid-swoop, taking out a table full of silver dishes and platters.

The swan hit the ground, rolling several feet until it came to a stop, struggling for breath.

Behind Ethan, Owen gave a chuckle. "Ah, I see you made it after all, Your Highness."

Ethan turned back to Owen with a confused frown. "What?"

Owen's lips curved into a dramatic pout. "Oh, innocent boy. Went and pledged your love to the wrong prince."

"What are you talking about?" Ethan asked, casting an uncertain glance back over his shoulder to where the swan lay gasping on the floor.

The imposter prince grinned and snapped his fingers. There was a flash of black lightning, and suddenly Raric stood where the black-dressed Owen had just been. The crowd gasped. Ethan's eyes flared wide, staring at the magician, then over at the swan that was struggling on the ground. Several guards were slowly moving toward the creature, as if unsure if they should help, but Ethan waved his hand sharply. "Don't touch him!" he ordered before he leaped the stairs and sprinted over to the fallen swan, dropping to his knees and scooping it up. The feathered body felt like nothing in his arms, and Ethan could feel an icy coldness already spreading. "Owen," he begged softly. "It's you, isn't it?" The swan's eyes turned upward, the light in them already starting to fade. It rubbed its downy head under Ethan's chin as it trembled in his arms. "You're going to be all right," Ethan said firmly, holding him close to his chest. He turned back to Raric. "The vow I made was for him."

Raric spread his hands wide from his sides, and the crowd gave an involuntary surge back. "Not how it works, I'm afraid."

Ethan glanced down at the swan again, touching his cheek gently. "I won't let you die," he said before he lowered Owen carefully back to the floor, yanking the cape from his shoulders to wrap around him. He stood and turned toward Raric, fire in his dark eyes. "What do you want for his life?"

Raric threw back his head and laughed. Elistair started to motion to the guards, but Ethan held up a hand. "Leave him to me," he growled. The guards wavered, looking over at Elistair for confirmation. They hesitated, then nodded at Ethan.

Ethan turned and stalked back to Raric. "If he dies, I will make you suffer."

"Is that a threat?" Raric asked with a wry smile.

Ethan grabbed Raric by the front of his shirt. "Yes."

Raric didn't even bother pushing Ethan's hands away. "So bloodthirsty, Your Highness. But killing me won't save your precious prince."

"What do you want to spare him?" Ethan asked bitterly.

Raric shrugged. "What are you willing to give me?"

Ethan glanced back at the swan on the floor. It was lying deathly still now, round eyes closed. His heart raced in his ears so much that he could barely hear his own voice. "Me," he said firmly, turning back to Raric again. "Let him live, and I will marry you. You can rule Comorra, by my side."

The room erupted into gasps and mumbling from the crowd, but Ethan ignored them, holding Raric's gaze. Raric stared at him before a lazy smirk crossed his features. "Is that so?"

"I give you my word," Ethan said determinedly. "You can have my kingdom if you let him live. Thornwood and Comorra, both under your rule."

Raric looked thoughtful for a moment, but whatever he had been planning to say was cut short as there was a sudden swirl of black light around the swan's prostrate form. It lifted the limp bird from the ground, Ethan's cape falling away. The magic swirled around the swan before surging inward and then out again. A bright flash later, and Owen lay curled on the ballroom floor. He groaned weakly, lifting his head, his face no longer bloodless and gaunt. Ethan turned and rushed to him, dropping to his knees next to him to help Owen sit up.

Owen glanced down at his hands. The strange thrum of dark magic that had filled his body since Raric had cursed him was gone, and for the first time since then, he felt wholly himself again. He looked up at Ethan, blue eyes shimmering. "You... you would have given up your kingdom for me?" he asked.

"Of course, I would," Ethan said, reaching up to touch Owen's cheek. "I love you. Even if we weren't together, I'd want you to be alive and happy."

Owen's hand found Ethan's on his face, pressing tightly. "An act of eternal love," he said softly.

Ethan blinked, then smiled. "Forever, for you," he promised.

Behind them, Raric let out a snarl as he realized the curse had lifted from Owen. "No!"

Ethan pointed viciously at Raric. "Arrest him," he ordered. The guards surged forward. Raric roared and gathered a ball of lightning into his hand. He threw it down, and it exploded in a brilliant burst that sent waves of crackling lightning through the room. Every window of the ballroom shattered; dust and smoke billowing outwards in a shockwave that knocked nearly everyone in the room to the floor. Ethan threw himself over Owen as glass and debris flew.

Out of the center of the chaos rose a gigantic dragon, black as night, with blood red horns and leathery wings that unfurled with a snap like thunder. Standing on its hind legs, the beast's head nearly touched the chandeliers above. It opened its jaws, revealing rows of massively sharp teeth. The roar that came from its throat was deafening, shaking the stone walls of the palace, and the wedding guests scattered for the ballroom doors.

The dragon's tail swung around and knocked over a table, sending cutlery and chunks of wood flying. "Captain!" Ethan called. "Protect the monarch and the guests!"

Captain Xan didn't even take time to respond, simply throwing a hasty salute to Ethan as he turned and pointed his guards toward the dais where Elistair and Sonia were, and another group toward some partygoers who seemed frozen in place with fear.

Ethan turned to Owen. "Run and hide," he said firmly. "I won't let him hurt you."

Owen glanced down at the sword on Ethan's hip, the only weapon he currently had, then up into his dark eyes. "What about you?"

"I'll be fine," Ethan assured him. "I need you to help protect Nomy and the guests. Please."

Owen gave him a quick kiss, then turned and dashed to where the guards had made a protective circle around Monarch Elistair and Princess Sonia. "Quickly, Your Highnesses," the guard said, motioning for them to exit out one of the side doors further into the castle.

"Go," Sonia said, giving Elistair and Owen a push. "I'm going to help get the guests to safety."

"I'll help you," Owen said, and Sonia did not argue with him. The guards hurried Elistair from the room as Sonia moved to direct the people who were all trying to rush out the doors.

The dragon reared its head and opened its long snout. Ethan saw black crackles of heat deep inside its gullet, and for a moment, his mind went blank. Hunting and sparring were one thing, but this was a real fight, one that he could very easily lose. He tried to move, but his feet suddenly felt like lead weights as Raric let loose a torrent of black flames right at him. He thought the impact that sent him flying was the flames until he hit the ground, and Xan landed on top of him. He could feel the intensity of the fire blast blister his skin and singe his hair. Raric roared, whipping his tail around again, and the flames spread in an arc, catching anything flammable in its wake. Xan rolled away from the dragon's stampeding feet, scrambling to get out of the path of the black flames that made the air shimmer with heat. Sonia sprinted to his side, dropping to her knees and quickly beating away the embers that clung to his skin and armor.

The black flames surrounded Ethan, trapping him in a ring with Raric, and he felt like his skin might start to melt off his bones from the intensity of the heat. Raric's tail lashed at him, another stream of fire erupting from his mouth, but this time, Ethan did not allow himself to freeze. He sprinted underneath Raric to protect himself from the black flames. He glanced up to see that the scales on the underside of Raric's body were much less thick than the ones on his back and were also spaced wider apart. He shoved the steel of his sword upward, and it penetrated the softer scales, sinking in to the hilt.

The dragon screamed and stomped, and Ethan was nearly trampled as Raric lashed around, trying to find him. The dragon stood up on its hind legs again, the hilt of Ethan's sword protruding from its lower belly. It snarled and tried to pull the sword out, but its front appendages were not meant for such coordinated efforts. Ethan looked around frantically for a dropped sword or dagger or spear, anything else to defend himself as the dragon's blood-red eye turned toward him. Something glimmered in the heat waves, and Ethan dove for it. It was a bow, dropped by one of the guards in the chaos. Ethan reached for his quiver on his back, then remembered with despair that he did not currently have it.

Owen cast a frantic glance around, trying to find something that might be helpful. Debris was everywhere, and anything that might be of use was being scattered by people running. He looked up to see Xan hand Sonia his own bow, and Sonia looked desperately around.

There was a smattering of arrows scattered across the floor, most of them trampled from fleeing guests, but Owen closed his hand around one that was unbroken, getting to his feet and dashing over to Sonia, shoving people out of his way to reach her.

The dragon's mouth pulled back into a fearsome grin, all of its teeth showing. He snapped at Ethan, and the prince felt the pressure from the dragon's jaws as he dove aside again.

"Ethan!" He heard the shout from Sonia somewhere behind him. He turned toward the sound, barely able to make out his sister through the dancing flames. She had a bow in her hand, loaded with a single arrow. Ethan caught her eye and nodded. Sonia let it loose with a sharp twang. The arrow sailed through the ring of fire. Ethan reached out and caught it, nocking it into his own bow as he turned, lifted it to his shoulder, and fired. The sharp tip of the arrow pierced through the scales on Raric's chest. Raric screamed, the sound causing the entire building to shake. He stumbled backward, tail lashing and flailing. He struck Ethan with it, and the prince went flying through the flames, hitting the floor outside of them with a pained grunt, quickly rolling to extinguish the fire that had ignited his clothes.

Raric staggered, great droplets of crimson blood falling from the wound where Ethan's arrow had pierced directly into his heart. With a crash that reverberated like a thunderclap, his enormous scaly body hit the floor, his chin the last bit to fall, and he lay still. After a moment, a surge of wind emanated out from where he landed, extinguishing the black flames and knocking everyone in the room off their feet. The dragon melted away until all that remained was the body of the once great dark magician in the middle of the floor in a widening pool of blood.

Sonia scrambled up and held out her hand to Owen. He took it, then glanced over at where Ethan lay on the floor, unmoving. He dashed to his side, dropping to his knees as he cradled Ethan's head in his hands. "Ethan! Wake up!"

Nothing moved, and Owen felt tears start to glide down his cheeks. Then Ethan's eyelids fluttered, and he winced, curling into a ball against Owen's torso. "Ouch," he groaned, cradling his arm close.

Owen's breath came out in a burst of laughter, and he wrapped his arms around Ethan, hugging him tightly. "You're alive!"

Ethan opened his eyes, then winced and shut them again. "Of course. I could never leave you." Owen squeezed him close, and Ethan groaned. "Too... tight..."

Owen quickly let go, shifting for Ethan to lean against him. Sonia hurried over. "Ethan!"

Ethan's dark eyes cracked open to look up blearily at his sister. "Thank you."

Sonia dropped a kiss onto his forehead, then frowned at the unnatural angle of his arm. "I'm going to get Lady Tsume."

"I'll be all right," Ethan said, groaning as he buried his face in Owen's chest. "Treat anyone worse than me first."

Sonia nodded and hurried away. Owen stroked Ethan's hair lovingly. "Breathe," he prompted. "I'm here."

"Are you all right?" Ethan asked, reaching up his unbroken arm to hold Owen's cheek.

"Yes," Owen said gently. "I'm just fine, thanks to you."

Ethan gave him a tired smile, glancing over to see Tsume approaching by Sonia's side, looking none the worse for wear. She stopped and bent over Xan, where the captain was nursing a nasty burn on his leg, her withered hands outstretched as magic began to flow from her palm over the damaged skin.

"By the way," Owen said, drawing his attention back again. Owen's pretty, sapphire eyes were narrowed in disapproval at him. "I would be remiss if I didn't tell you that offering to let Raric rule Comorra with you was an incredibly foolish thing for you to do. It would have been terrible for your country and your people."

"I couldn't lose you," Ethan defended, but Owen wrapped his arms around him.

"I know. I'm glad you did it, even if it was foolish." And then Owen kissed him, cupping Ethan's cheeks in his palms. Ethan kissed him eagerly back. Owen pressed their foreheads together. "But please, don't do that again just for me. Our kingdoms need us to be strong rulers."

"And we will be. Together," Ethan said as Tsume hurried up to him.

She gave the blond a small smile. "You must be Prince Owen."

"Yes," Owen said, giving her a gracious nod of his head.

"This is Lady Tsume," Ethan said as the old woman took his injured arm in her hand. "She helped me find you. I wouldn't have known where to even start without her."

"I am forever grateful to you, Lady Tsume," Owen said, giving her a bright smile.

Tsume clucked her tongue lightly. "Magic should always be used for good, Your Highness," she said before she bowed her head and spoke a few words over Ethan's arm, her knobby fingers tracing the broken bone gently. Ethan winced, but a moment later, his arm straightened, and the swelling went down until it looked the same as it always did.

Owen beamed. "That is amazing. You have a gift, Lady Tsume."

Tsume smiled. "I am glad to help where I can, Your Highness. I must go see to the other wounded if you are both well enough."

"Yes, please do," Ethan said, giving his arm an experimental bend. "It feels great."

Tsume nodded and stood, hurrying away to another group of people. Owen touched Ethan's arm lightly. "Magic is wonderful. It will be a pity when it's gone."

"I won't miss it," Ethan said, stroking Owen's hair back from his eyes lovingly. "I'd break every bone in my body to save you." Somehow, Owen didn't doubt that.

A sudden scream had both of their heads shooting up, and Owen watched people scatter backwards, women lifting their skirts out of the way, as a furry figure came running across the floor. Alli came to a stop in front of him, Sir William perched on her back like a noble knight. "Owen!" she cried and launched herself into his arms. Owen caught her and hugged her tightly.

"Thank you, Alli, Sir William!" He gave the salamander's head a pat. "I couldn't have done this without you."

Alli nuzzled her head under his chin, then looked over at Ethan. "Is this your man?"

Ethan stared at her in surprise, then flushed. "Um... you're the otter I tried to shoot the other night, aren't you?"

"I am," Alli said with a slight huff.

Ethan held out his hand toward her. "I am so sorry. I know now that you were protecting Owen, and for that, I am forever in your debt."

Alli gave his hand a shake with her paw. "I'm just glad he's safe and back with you, Ethan. No hard feelings."

"Thank you," Ethan said gratefully. He glanced at Sir William, who nodded his head at him from Alli's back. "And who is this?"

"This is Willie," Alli said as the lizard slid off her back to the ground.

"SIR William Farthington, at your service, Your Highness," Sir William said, kneeling on one knee.

"He and Alli are my best friends and helped protect me from Raric," Owen said.

"Then you also have my eternal gratitude," Ethan said, giving Sir William a smile.

Sir William nodded, then turned to Owen. "I wonder, Your Majesty, now that your spell has been broken, if I might perhaps impose upon you?"

"Oh," Owen said, glancing over at Ethan, then back to Sir William. "Do you think it will work with Raric dead?"

"Only one way to find out," Alli said.

Owen hesitated, then held out his hand, and Sir William crawled up onto it. Owen lifted the salamander to his mouth and dropped a kiss on his tiny head.

Nothing happened.

Sir William's face fell a bit. "Ah. It seems not," he said with a resigned sigh.

Ethan frowned. "What is it?"

Owen gave Ethan a sorrowful look. "Sir William was cursed by Raric to be a salamander until he's kissed by a virgin."

Ethan frowned. "But you're not a virgin."

"You're not?" Sir William asked in surprise, and Owen blushed. "Sorry, I didn't know how to say it."

"Well, no wonder it didn't work," Alli said with a slight huff.

"What is this about being a virgin?" Sonia suddenly asked as she came up to them, eyeing the otter on the floor and the salamander in Owen's hand curiously.

"This is Sir William. He was cursed to be a salamander until he gets kissed by a virgin," Owen said, holding up the lizard. "My kiss didn't work."

"Well, of course not," Sonia said with a chuckle, glancing over at Ethan with a look that made her brother turn bright red. She held out her hand. "Here."

Owen blinked in surprise, but he held Sir William out for him to crawl into Sonia's hand. She lifted the salamander to her mouth and gave him a smooch on the nose. His pupils went wide, and his feet suddenly rose off of Sonia's hand. There was a swirl of wind and dark lightning around him, and then there stood a man of middle years, with short, dark hair, round brown eyes, and a large, thick moustache. And he was naked.

Sir William stared down at himself in surprise, lifting his hands to blink at them as Sonia blushed and clapped her hand to her mouth. He glanced down, then quickly cupped his hands over his genitals, flushing. "My sincerest apologies, my lady!" he said, waddling backwards a few steps until he found Ethan's discarded cape and quickly wrapped it around himself.

Sonia giggled softly. "It's all right, Sir William."

"I am forever in your debt," Sir William said, lowering himself to his knees, adjusting his makeshift cover carefully. "I pledge to serve you and your family for the rest of my life, if you wish it."

"We can discuss that after we find you some proper clothes," Sonia said in her most magnanimous voice.

Sir William blushed, then turned to Owen and Ethan. "I am eternally grateful to you, Your Majesty," he said, taking Owen's hand to press a kiss to the back of it.

Owen smiled softly. "I am just glad I could help you, Sir William. What about you, Alli?" He turned to the little otter.

Alli shrugged. "I don't need anything."

"Would you like to stay with us in the palace?" Ethan offered. "I'm sure it would be more comfortable and safer than living out in the wild."

Alli blinked, then beamed at him. "If that would be all right."

"Of course!" Ethan said, and Owen grinned. "We'll even create your own space for you."

"Could it lead out to the moat?" Alli asked, hope shining in her black button eyes.

"Absolutely!" Ethan said with a grin.

Alli gave an excited, little hop. "Oh, thank you, Ethan! I would love that."

"Alli! Address His Highness with the propriety he deserves!" Sir William said pointedly, which both of the princes seemed to find amusing coming from a man with almost no clothes on.

Alli blinked, but Owen shook his head. "It's all right. Without you, I wouldn't be here. You can call us by our names as much as you want."

Alli giggled and suddenly zoomed up Owen's torso to curl around his neck, her whiskers tickling his cheek. "You're the best, Owen!"

Monarch Elistair suddenly hurried up to them, Xan following, barely limping on his mostly-healed leg. Elistair dropped to their knees, wrapping Ethan in a hug with one arm, and Owen in the other. "My boys," they said softly. "Are you all right?"

"Yes, Nomy," Ethan said, hugging Elistair tightly. "You?"

"Just fine, my love," Elistair said, pressing a kiss to Ethan's forehead. They turned to Owen, reaching up to touch his cheek. "I am so sorry I did not have faith that you were still alive, Owen."

Owen shook his head, holding their hand to his face. "It's all right, Your Majesty. I am here again with all of you."

Elistair nodded, pressing a kiss to Owen's forehead too, then gave Alli's head a light scritch before pulling back. "There is much to be done," they said, glancing around at the ruined main hall, with charred wood, overturned tables, and the body of the dark magician still lying in the middle of the floor. "I do not wish you to rush into marriage if you do not want to, now that the spell has been lifted."

Owen glanced over at Ethan, who smiled softly at him. "I still want to marry you," he said, reaching up to stroke Owen's cheek. "But what do you want?"

"I still want to marry you too," Owen said, tears shimmering in his eyes. "But let us see that our people are tended to, and everything is set right again, so that we may celebrate without any hesitation."

Ethan nodded, leaning in to kiss him. "Of course." He turned to Xan. "What can we do to help, Captain?"

Epilogue

It was several months before the castle was safely repaired and completed. In that time, Elistair and Sonia ensured that those injured in Raric's attack were cared for by Tsume and the kingdom physicians. Sir William contacted his family in Thornwood, who rejoiced at him being alive. Sir William then accompanied Owen and Ethan back to Thornwood. Without the rulers, some aspects of Thornwood flourished, while others languished. Owen and Ethan, along with many of King Stephan's loyal advisors and knights, reorganized to help ensure the stability of the kingdom and its subjects. The people mourned the passing of good King Stephan and Queen Amelia, but they celebrated the coronation of King Owen and his engagement to Prince Ethan, and there was much festivity throughout the land.

The cold months came, and Owen and Ethan settled in for the winter at the Thornwood palace, with plans to return to Comorra in the spring, where they would officially be married and unite their kingdoms. They curled up together in front of a roaring fire, arms around each other as if they would never let go again.

"Will you love me forever?" Owen asked, his eyes shining as Ethan held him close.

"No," Ethan said, caressing his cheek gently. "Far, far longer than that."

He did. And they both lived happily ever after.

Acknowledgements

Thank you for reading my first foray into writing Young Adult. I am so glad I was able to take such a nostalgic story and turn it into a fairy tale that hopefully resonates with readers of all ages!

Thank you to my adult beta readers: Michelle, Mozz, Avril, Amanda, and Sharon. And an extra big thank you to Kennedy Sutton for reading multiple drafts and helping me develop the story while procrastinating on her own projects!

And to my younger beta readers, Caitlyn and Michael, thank you for giving me your unique perspectives! You can now brag to your friends that you were thanked by an author in a book. Have a dragon.

About the Author

Kit Barrie (she/her) was raised by pirates in a traveling carnival where she learned how to fly and to weave fantasy into reality. She identifies as chaotic bisexual, with good intentions and questionable methods. She lives in an utterly unfantastical state in the Midwestern United States with her very supportive spouse (VSS) and at least 4 food goblins who might just be cats gobblin' food.

Please visit www.kitbarrie.com or scan the QR code below for more information on Kit and her other available titles.